TRUST IN ME

Melody Hepworth is made redundant from her job in London, and has parted from her boyfriend. She returns home to the small Devon town where her Aunt Cis runs an antiques business. A lover of vintage clothes, Mel decides to start collecting them again and make a new career, turning the shabby old shop into a sophisticated modern boutique. When she meets attractive local silversmith Rick Martin, there's a spark — but Mel knows she will never trust a man again, let alone allow herself to love him . . .

CHRISTINA GREEN

---◆---

TRUST IN ME

Complete and Unabridged

LINFORD
Leicester

First published in Great Britain in 2014

First Linford Edition
published 2015

A catalogue record for this book is available
from the British Library.

ISBN 978–1–4448–2623–4

Published by
F. A. Thorpe (Publishing)
Anstey, Leicestershire

Set by Words & Graphics Ltd.
Anstey, Leicestershire
Printed and bound in Great Britain by
T. J. International Ltd., Padstow, Cornwall

This book is printed on acid-free paper

1

I entered the shop and at once her smile greeted me. Little Aunt Cecilia, plump and still pretty, behind her counter, knitting and listening to some quiet music from the radio at her side. I put down my bag and went towards her.

'Hallo, Aunt Cis. It's lovely to see you, and so kind of you to let me come and stay for a bit.'

Her busy fingers dropped the knitting and her smile grew even more welcoming.

'Oh, Mel, you know you're always welcome — and truly, I'm glad to have you.' The smile faded a bit. 'You see, I have one or two problems which I'm sure you can help me with.'

I heard the drop in the voice and knew that she was unhappy. Well, here I was, begging a few weeks' stay with my loving godmother and aunt, so I was in the right place. Yes, we would sort out all the problems — hers and mine, too.

I put my arms around her, warm and soft, just as she was when I was a child and I knew I would do whatever I could to keep her safe from any undue worries.

I pulled up a chair beside her, and said quietly, 'Well, the shop looks good, Aunt Cis — stocked well with your lovely porcelain and glass, I should say — and that little jewellery showcase full of exciting bits and pieces. So what's the problem?'

She sighed, folded her knitting into a neat pile which she put beneath the counter, and met my eyes.

'Do you remember Nigel Payne, my Denys's younger cousin? I think you met him once or twice when you lived here.'

I thought back. I had come to live with Aunt Cis when my parents had died in a plane crash, all of fifteen years ago. She had been a surrogate mother to me as I grew up. It had been Aunt

Cis who had encouraged me to find a trade I enjoyed. I had lived in London for the last six and a half years, running a small business with my friend Lissa Newton, selling vintage clothes. I stopped thinking then, knowing that my own problems with Lissa must be put away for the time being, for it was important to resolve Aunt Cis's troubles first. So — Nigel Payne . . .

'Yes,' I said, frowning. 'I do remember him. Much younger than Uncle Denys, tall and not bad-looking but a bit wild, if I remember rightly. Uncle Denys was quiet and thoughtful and lovely, but Nigel was different.'

'Indeed he was different. And he's even more so now.'

I looked at her anxious face.

'You've seen him lately?'

She shook her head.

'No, but I had a letter out of the blue a few weeks ago, asking if he could come to stay as he was looking for a new start in life.' She stopped, looked at me and added, almost in an undertone,

'And I knew at once he was trouble.'

'Trouble, Aunt Cis? In what way?'

I saw her hands shaking, so took them in mine and she smiled for a moment. Then: 'I think he's after my business, that's what.'

I caught my breath. Bartlett Antiques, the business that Uncle Denys and Aunt Cis had run for a very long time — happily and successfully — was, I thought, still continuing. It certainly provided Aunt Cis with an income, and a reason for living now that she was alone after Denys's death two years ago; and I had heard from the family and local friends that it did very well. It had an excellent reputation and attracted dealers and tourists from far and wide. I frowned. So perhaps Nigel had heard all this on the local gossip line and decided that this was his new start in life.

I said firmly, 'Well, I'm here to support you, Aunt Cis. Between us, we'll sort it out.' I gave her a broad smile and saw, with relief, that her own answered it.

4

'Well,' she said, 'that's made me feel much better, Mel. Now, why don't we have a cup of coffee, and then you can tell me all your news.'

'What a good idea. I'll go and put the kettle on.' I left her reaching once more for the knitting, and went through the little back room into the kitchen which was just as I remembered it: warm, shabby and full of cooking scents, with some of Uncle Denys's paintings on the walls. As I made the coffee, I thought about that wretched Nigel Payne and knew I would tell him a few home truths when he came back; which I guessed he could do at any time. Well, I was ready for him!

We drank our coffee and ate a few of Aunt Cis's delectable flapjacks while she asked me about my life up in the big smoke.

'Last time you came down you seemed so happy. You said you were doing well with the old clothes.'

'Vintage, please, Aunt Cis — quite a bit better than old clothes, you know!'

We had a good laugh and then she said quietly, 'And you have a lovely boyfriend, don't you, Mel? I don't recall his name, but . . . '

I reached for another flapjack and said quickly, 'That was Tony. I'm afraid we split last year.'

I saw shock on her lined face, and realized that today's world was light years away from her own.

'We're still good friends, Aunt Cis. But he was working away from London, and I was so busy, even at weekends, with festivals and fashion shows, that we hardly ever met. We decided it was no good. We couldn't go on like that, so . . . '

I stopped and bit my lip. It had been so hard, losing Tony, with his laughter and understanding, but the break had been a friendly and clean one, and I told myself I was getting over it. After all, lots of other couples these days had the same sort of problematic lives and lived through them. All I had to do was get out and about and find a new job.

Aunt Cis must have read some of those thoughts. She stirred her coffee and then, with love shining in her faded eyes, said gently, 'You'll meet someone else, Mel, of course you will. You're a good, kind girl and any man would be thankful to be part of your life. Just wait for it to happen, love.'

The lump in my throat grew bigger and I had to swallow the dregs of coffee to make it go. Yes, I knew what Aunt Cis was hoping for, but I didn't think it would happen. For, after leaving me, Tony had lost no time in finding a new partner, and that had hurt me very much. So much, that I wondered if I would ever love, or trust, another man. Tony's love for me had become the backbone of my life, and he had let it die a quick death once we parted. Now, I had decided that no other man would ever persuade me to take that dangerous step and commit myself again.

I avoided Aunt Cis's knowledgeable eyes and changed the subject.

'Do you still do the market on a

Friday? If so, may I come with you? I'm sure there'll be a few interesting things to look at.'

I saw from her expression that she understood my sudden surge of emotions; bless her, she just smiled and said, 'Certainly we'll go. It'll be good to have your company, Mel, love.'

We packed a few smallish things into the same old green van that I recalled from several years ago and Aunt Cis drove us very correctly and rather slowly up the hill into the square where the stalls spread out. I saw that she became slightly breathless with all the effort, and was glad to sit down when we reached her stall. It was a bare trestle table, with a couple of stools pushed underneath, but she smiled as she relaxed, and called a greeting to the man in the next stall.

'Morning, Fred. Quite a crowd already — should be a good day.'

Fred, red-faced and with huge, drooping shoulders, came to her side, grinning.

'Sunshine bringing us luck as well as holidaymakers, eh, Cis? What we need, ain't it. And who's this with you?'

I smiled at him and said, 'I'm Mel. Cis is my aunt; I'm just here for a break, but I'll do what I can to help.'

He nodded, walked back to his own stall, and then looked back at me, beckoning with one large finger.

I went to his side.

'What is it, Fred?'

'Just a word, lover. Yer aunt's a feisty lady but I sometimes think this selling lark's getting too much for her. See, she gets breathless at times, she does. Just wanted you to know.'

I looked back at Aunt Cis, saw how she was breathing more normally now, taking off her coat and chatting with an elderly lady on the other side of her stall. She looked all right I thought, but as both Fred and I had seen the breathlessness, then something must be done about it. I resolved to do all I could to help her to keep the business going. The years were flying by, as I knew with my own life. Well, I would look after Aunt Cis, now that I was here; I might even suggest it was time to bring in someone to help. Nigel Payne, whispered a small voice in my head, and I said out loud, without thinking, 'Oh, no, not him!'

Aunt Cis looked at me as she got up from her stool and began to arrange small things on the trestle table, which she had already covered with a nice green brocade cloth. 'What did you say, Mel? So much noise going on I didn't quite hear.'

I joined her, lifting the heavier pieces onto the table for her. 'Nothing, Aunt Cis, just talking to myself. My word, yes, it certainly is noisy here — and, oh look, here's someone coming around with a tray of coffee. Just what we need! I'll get a couple of mugs, shall I?'

I left her arranging Victorian bracelets and earrings and pottery and glass and knew she'd be quite happy now that everything was in front of her and not needing any more physical effort.

I moved away from the stall, towards the man with the tray who stood at the far end of the square. So many people here now, selling so many different things. I passed terrifying African masks, smiled at the heaps of pristine white Victorian linen on another stall, and lots of china and glass, and wondered if I might take a few minutes to look at the rails of second-hand clothes and see if I could pick up an interesting vintage dress or hat. In fact, I was so busy thinking that I didn't really notice where I was going, and I stepped right into the pathway of a burly figure, causing his mug of coffee to slop over him. A deep voice said, 'Look where you're going, can't you?' and I looked into irate pale blue eyes that held an icy chip, lightening up a frowning, suntanned face.

I blushed, which was ridiculous at my age, but I knew I should have had my wits about me, rather than daydreaming, as I so often did. I whipped off my scarf and handed it to the man in front

11

of me, and said breathlessly, 'Sorry, all my fault. Just wipe it off and I'll get you another mug.' I ran through the crowd towards the man with the tray who very plainly had just finished his round.

There was no coffee left. I said, 'Can you get some more?' and was told sharply: 'Go into the café if you want some. My round's done, and I'm off now to the next job.' Ashamed, I returned to the man still wiping his shirt sleeve, and then looking down at the broken china at his feet.

'No more coffee,' I said apologetically, and met those cold eyes again. 'I'll just get a brush and move those bits,' I added. 'Can't leave them lying about, can we?'

Not waiting for an answer, I returned to Aunt Cis's stall and grabbed the small dustpan and brush which lay among the unsorted wrapping bits.

'Back in a moment,' I told her. 'Had a small accident, must just put things right and then I'll be with you again.'

If I expected to be rebuked, I was

wrong. Dear Aunt Cis chuckled and said lightly, 'Go on, love, sort it out and then have yourself a look around. I'll be all right here for a few hours. Just go and enjoy yourself.'

I was about to say no, I'm supposed to be helping you, when that deep voice said, close behind me, 'What about a cup in the café? Sorry I was so sharp — coffee on me, yes?'

Turning, I discovered the icy blue eyes were bright and smiling. I blinked. I hadn't expected this. But, despite the old feeling of not wanting to spend time with any particular man, suddenly it seemed a very nice idea.

I smiled back, said, 'I'd like that.' Looking around I saw the café sign. 'Over there,' I said, and led the way through groups of milling, chattering market workers.

2

We sat at a small table beside the window, and my new acquaintance went to collect mugs of coffee and a couple of chocolate biscuits.

'My way of saying sorry,' he said with a big smile, when he brought both back to the table. 'I was miles away when you bumped into me — just as much my fault. So — my name's Rick Martin, what's yours?'

'Melody Hepworth. Call me Mel.' I looked at him very keenly. A lived-in face but with strength written into the lines and the chiselled jaw. An untidy mane of dark hair fell to just below his collar, while an uncontrollable fringe bounced over pale blue eyes, showcasing a smile that could charm birds from the trees. Careful, Mel, I told myself, sipping coffee and accepting a biscuit. I watched him stir sugar into his mug and waited for a reply. It came with an even more handsome smile than I'd seen so far, and a definite twinkle in those perceptive eyes.

'Melody! Can I persuade you to sing for your supper — or your morning coffee?'

I said, firmly, 'I don't sing. I collect vintage clothes. And what do you do, Rick Martin?'

He pulled a dilapidated notebook out of his jacket pocket, opened it and slid it across the table.

'I'm a silversmith. I make jewellery. Here are some of my designs.'

I was intrigued. I'd met jewellery craftsmen in London, but never an actual silversmith. And certainly not one who designed things in a ratty-looking notebook. Opening a page I looked at a neatly drawn sketch of what I took to be a brooch, consisting, I supposed, of gems and some sort of solid setting. It stood out, and I knew I would love to see the finished article. Talent, I thought, and was impressed.

Pushing the notebook back over the table, I said, 'Do you practise your trade here in Stretton? I suppose you have a studio somewhere.'

'In my dreams!' he said, laughing. 'I only wish I had. I have a room in someone else's workshop. I could do better if I had my own place. As it is, I have to put up with Gary's choice of music, and a lot of chatter when I'm trying to concentrate.'

We looked at each other across the table. By now both mugs were empty and I supposed I should really return to Aunt Cis and see how she was getting on. But then, out of the blue, a woman pounced upon Rick, putting her hands on his shoulders and pulling him around to face her.

'Rick! Sweetheart! Knew I'd find you somewhere here. I've just come from the lady of the manor, you know, Mrs Sothern. She needs a new silver bracelet for her daughter's birthday. Said I'd tell you to call on her — soon. She'll give you a splendid commission, I'm sure.'

Amused, I watched Rick's expression change from surprise to what seemed to be amusement.

He rose, led the speaker to my side, and said, 'Here's someone else you can find commissions for, Allegra — this is Melody, and she's into vintage clothes. With all your contacts, surely you know a good source in the town you could introduce her to?'

He winked at me, and the blue eyes twinkled even more merrily.

'Mel, meet Allegra Smith, who runs the town's communications centre. In fact, she *is* the communications centre!'

'Oh, you naughty boy!' Allegra wrapped her floaty scarf more tightly around her neck, frowned at Rick then gave me a devastating smile.

'Don't believe a word he says, my dear — but yes, of course I know a few stallholders you could call on.'

She looked around, then added, 'Why, Sue Bennett, just over there — the stall with those gorgeous satin blouses hanging up. Come along, I'll introduce you. Melody, is that your name? Oh, delightful! Rick, go and see Mrs Sothern at once. Mel, come with me . . . '

We were both quickly shooed away from the table and the empty mugs, Rick looking at me with a raised eyebrow, and then waving a salute as he headed for the high arch at the far end of the market which led into the town itself. I followed Allegra and her colourful, floating dress through people who turned, grinned, and passed the time of day, until we reached Sue Bennett's stall.

'Now, Sue, my dear, here's Melody who would like to look at your vintage clothes. I'm sure she'll give you a good price for anything she fancies. I'll leave you to it — I have so much to do today.' Waving a hand in farewell, she gave us a huge smile, then turned and disappeared off through the crowded market.

I took a deep breath, looked at Sue, who was middle-aged, well dressed and with a face that told stories of a hard life.

'Well,' she said, 'that's Allegra Smith for you, always telling people how to live their lives.'

Her smile broadened, and I responded to it.

'I'm pleased to meet you, Sue. My name's Melody Hepworth. Mel to my friends.'

'Nice to know you. By all means have a look around the rails. I've got a few rather lovely old things. Got a stall of your own, have you?' She pointed at the rail at the back of her stall and I started pushing clothes along it, mostly old and faded, and certainly not what I was looking for.

'No,' I said. 'I worked in London for six years but now I've been made redundant. I'm staying with my aunt who runs the antique stall over there.'

'Oh yes, Mrs Bartlett. She has some lovely things. She's a great old girl. Here, have a look at this.'

From beneath the trestle table she produced a box and opened it. Out fell a beautiful Devore evening jacket, loose sleeves, draped bodice, glittering royal blue with a dark green weave running through it.

'Edwardian,' she said. 'Try it on, there's a mirror over there.'

I did so and was caught at once. The jacket was elegance itself. Quality and beauty — I had to have it.

'How much, Sue?' I asked.

She smiled and named a sum that I knew was right for such a luxury item, but my business sense made me shake my head, and hand the jacket back to her.

'Too much, I'm afraid. If I'm going to start my own business . . . ' And was I? It was the first I'd heard of it! ' . . . I need to consolidate my finances.'

She thought for a moment, and then said, 'I'd like us to be friends, Mel. So you can have it with my good wishes and a tenner off. Here, love, take it. We've all got to help one another in this trade, you know.'

I accepted the jacket, now safely back again in the wrapped box, paid for it and then looked along the rest of the rails.

'I'm very grateful, Sue. It's lovely to have met you and had a bit of a chat. I left everybody I knew in London, you see.'

She nodded. 'I'll look forward to seeing you again. Keep in with Allegra — she's odd, but she has so many useful contacts. And local gossip is always handy, isn't it?'

I smiled at her. 'Yes,' I said. And I meant it. Perhaps gossip might keep me in touch with that talented silversmith, Rick Martin. I returned to Aunt Cis's stall with the smile still on my face.

She was selling something small but expensive to an American tourist who kept haggling. I sat down quietly and watched my soft-hearted, often senti-mental aunt acting out the part of a business-like seller, and admired her very much. And I realized too, seeing the life on her lined face and hearing the energy in her voice, that Aunt Cis would never be ready to retire from her beloved antique business.

We drove back down the hill and reopened the shop.

'I only ever leave it for one morning a week,' she told me as she stirred soup on the stove. 'Perhaps you'd go and remove the Closed notice, Mel, would you? I don't want customers to think I'm shut all day.'

'Of course.'

I went through the small back room and straight to the door. The morning post had arrived before we left for the market, but now a piece of crumpled paper lay on the floor just inside the door. I changed the notice, picked up the paper and made my way back to the kitchen. But curiosity made me look at the sketchy writing on the paper, and I gasped as I read the message.

'*Disappointed to find you closed, but will be back late when hopefully you'll be open again. Looking forward to seeing you,*' and then the scrawled signature, '*Nigel.*'

I gave the paper to Aunt Cis who was

slicing bread at the kitchen table. She put down the knife, frowned, screwed up her eyes and read the message aloud. When she reached the name, she let the paper drop, looked at me and sighed a huge sigh.

'Oh dear,' she said, and then sank down into the waiting chair. After a moment, she got up again and moved the soup bowls nearer to the bubbling pan.

'I was so hoping he wouldn't come,' she said quietly. 'I know he's Denys's young cousin, but I also know he'll make trouble, Mel.' She looked at me with worried eyes. 'What do you think I should do? He'll want to stay, of course; after all, he said something about starting a new life and that means he's at a loose end. Well, I suppose he could always have the little box room, next to yours; it's not what I want, but what else can I do? I can't just turn him away, can I?'

I thought very hard and then said, 'You could, of course — tell him you're too old and busy to have to worry about other people, and perhaps suggest a local B and B. But I don't suppose you want to do that, do you, dear Aunt Cis? You're far too kind, you know.'

She put both bowls of soup on the table and sat down again. 'He's family,' she said, and I knew that was the end of the matter. Nigel would come, be welcomed, and he would sleep, warm and comfortable, in the box room. He would eat Aunt Cis's excellent meals and probably flirt with me. But could he really make trouble? To the extent that Aunt Cis feared, and which I could only imagine?

I took a spoonful of soup, smiled over the table and said, as lightly as I could, 'Let's hope for the best. We'll know a bit more when he comes. And don't worry, Aunt Cis, I can be pretty stroppy with difficult young men — working in London taught me that.'

I laughed so that she had to join in, and I was grateful to see the anxious expression disappear. I ate my soup slowly, thoughts very busy. Nigel would find a worthy adversary in me, even if Aunt Cis would be put to extra trouble and worry. I decided to spend the afternoon in the shop with her, doing one or two small jobs. Writing price labels, dusting shelves, and so on. I must be there when he came. And make sure he understood that the box room was only for a night or two and then he must get a move on, starting his famous new life.

By the time lunch was finished and the washing up done, I settled in with the odd jobs while Aunt Cis dealt with her accounts and read the catalogues which had come with the morning post. A few customers appeared, chatting and fingering small purchases, and one actually bought an expensive print.

And then, just as I was about to go into the kitchen and make a pot of tea, I heard the doorbell jangle, and in the doorway stood a young man with a big smile.

'Hiya!' he said, grinning first at me

and then at Aunt Cis, who stood up, pale-faced and unsmiling.

'Well, here I am, come to help you run this shop! Hi, Aunt Cis!'

Striding up to her, he threw his arms around her and kissed her surprised face.

I knew then that dealing with this enthusiastic intruder, reminding me painfully of Tony, who had left me in London, wouldn't be as easy as I had imagined.

3

'You must be Nigel,' I said, and at once he turned his attention to me.

'I am, which means Aunt Cis must have told you about me — so may I return the compliment: who are you?'

His voice was light and rapid and reminded me of London voices.

'Aunt Cis is my aunt and my godmother. My name is Melody . . . ' I stopped, because he was at my side, flecked brown eyes taking me in and grinning broadly.

'So we're related! Well, that's nice to know, and what a great name — Melody, as lovely as you are, if I may say so.'

Oh dear, I thought, just what I imagined might happen — flirting the very moment we met! I stepped away and kept a straight expression on my face.

'You didn't let me finish. Melody

Hepworth, and I've just left London for a few weeks, so I shan't be here very much longer.' And I hope that applies to you, too, I thought crossly. Then I caught Aunt Cis's glance and saw she was chuckling. Well at least she saw something humourous about this distant, cousinly intruder.

He turned again, looked around the shop and then said, still smiling, 'Seen better days, hasn't it, Aunt Cis? A long time since you and Uncle Denys started it all up — perhaps you'll let me help you jazz it up a bit.'

That was too much. I said firmly, 'This is a very well-known antique business, and I don't like the idea of it being changed, as I'm sure Aunt Cis doesn't.'

He shook his head. 'Times change you know, Melody. And we must change with them.'

Then Aunt Cis moved, pulled out something from behind the counter and I saw it was a padded envelope, addressed but not stamped. She smiled at him.

'You have a kind face, Nigel, so if you

really want to help, it would be good of you to deliver this to the Post Office, halfway up the hill on the left hand side. First Class and Recorded Delivery, please. And we'll have a cup of tea brewing by the time you come back.'

Poor Nigel. He clearly hadn't expected to be treated like a teenage errand boy. I watched his eyes narrow and his handsome face tighten, and wondered what he would do next. Refuse to go, perhaps? Or even walk away?

But he just sighed, said, 'Oh, er, all right ... ', took the envelope she handed him, and left the shop.

Aunt Cis and I stood there in silence, and then our eyes met and explosive laughter filled the shop around us.

'I don't believe it,' I said. 'He's just an overgrown little boy. We must get rid of him, Aunt, as soon as possible.'

For a moment she said nothing, but then she sat down, pulling some papers towards her and said, not looking at me, 'He's family, Mel. Just as you are. I can't send him away. We must just wait and see what happens next. Now, I'm going to have a good look at this catalogue, so forgive me if I keep quiet for a while.'

I knew she was right.

'Well,' I said, and paused. 'I suppose I'd better go and make up the bed in the box room. I hope he won't mind the birds scuffling about in the roof above. He'll just have to learn that Devon is different from London. All right, Aunt Cis, I'll be down again to make the tea.'

It took us a day or two to get used to the guest. Nigel was a busy sort of person, full of new ideas, and wanting to get out and about and look at places and meet people. But mostly he was interested in the shop. Which meant that Aunt Cis and I were always on the alert, wondering what he would come up with next. And he was interested in me, which I found slightly flattering but also rather irritating.

For instance he wanted to know what business I worked at in London.

'Something high up the scale, I bet,

Mel — you're that sort of a girl, aren't you?'

What could I say? I tightened my mouth and said shortly, 'I sold vintage clothes, that's all, and now I'm redundant, so I have to find something else to do.'

We were sitting at the supper table a few days after he had arrived. Aunt Cis was tired after a busy day of dealing with demanding customers, and I was wondering what on earth I would do if I didn't find a job down here in Stretton. In fact, I was also thinking about the interesting silversmith I had bumped into . . . I remembered his name, Rick Martin, and found myself dreamily imagining his warm smile and pale blue, all-seeing eyes. And, oh yes, that deeply vibrant voice that still echoed in my mind.

And then Nigel said, 'Well, why don't you start up a small stall for your old clothes — sorry, I mean vintage, of course! — right here in the shop. There's that little room behind the counter which would look great draped with fantastic, colourful clothes. And you could be there, dressed in a glittery, vintage-plus gown of some sort, ready to welcome all the rich American tourists. What do you think about that, Mel?'

I came out of my dream with a jerk and slopped the coffee I was drinking into my saucer.

'Rubbish!' I said forcefully. 'You don't know what you're talking about! For one thing, I have no stock; for another, Aunt Cis wouldn't want customers walking around her counter all the time, would she? Honestly, Nigel I think you're out of your mind.'

Silence, while he and I stared at each other across the table. But it was Aunt Cis who broke the charged atmosphere, saying in her quiet voice, 'Actually, it might be quite a good idea, Mel. Why not think about it? Today boutiques are all over the place, even here, in Stretton; fashionable little shops that seem to attract more and more customers. So why not use Nigel's idea to smarten up this shabby old place and call it something new and rather elegant, to do with antique pieces and vintage clothes?'

I felt myself quickening, thoughts whizzing around, and a glow starting in my toes, running all the way up to my ears. Yes, I thought, it could happen! I smiled at Aunt Cis.

'I might just consider it,' I said carefully, but she must have seen the excitement on my face, for she put her hand across the table and touched mine.

'My dear Mel, I would so love to have you here. Please don't say anything now, but just think about it. After all, you will have this property after I'm gone, so why not establish yourself just a bit earlier?'

She was smiling, laughing, and I felt emotions swirl inside me. And then I glanced at Nigel, saw the determination on his face, the gleam in his dark eyes, and knew I would have to play this very carefully.

Had he plans of taking on the shop himself? Well, if I decided to take up Aunt Cis's idea, then Nigel could be useful. But he would have to do things my way.

And then the sheer idea of showing off vintage clothes in this lovely old, paneled building, that small, atmospheric back room with scented candles, perhaps a few bits of bright jewellery giving life and light to the clothes, gave way to what I said next.

'As it happens, I did pick up a rather lovely jacket in the market when we were there — and I daresay there are more there. One of the stall holders — a nice woman, called Sue — said she would look out for likely things for me. Of course, it's only an idea, but, well, I might just do what you suggest, Aunt Cis.'

My excitement was growing.

'Look, I'll go and find that jacket I bought and you can say if you think it's the right sort of thing that would enhance your shop.'

I jumped up, left the room, raced up the narrow stairs, and found the jacket. I took it out of its box, put it on and went down into the kitchen. I stood in the open doorway.

'What do you think?'

Nigel whistled, which I ignored. But Aunt Cis looked with very keen eyes, and said at last, 'It's a beautiful thing, Mel, and wouldn't it look wonderful over a long dark skirt, or even floaty silk trousers, and perhaps a good piece of jewellery at your throat? Yes, love, if that's the sort of garment you want to sell, then I'm all in favour of our becoming a modern, elegant boutique. But, of course, it's for you to decide.'

That night I lay awake for what seemed hours, confusing thoughts running around my brain. If Aunt Cis and I turned old Bartlett Antiques into a more sophisticated little shop, selling both her porcelain and Victorian art and my clothes, then I would need stock, quickly. I remembered that Lissa, in London, had said as I left that she would be willing to let me have a few pieces at cost price. Would she still feel the same? And then there was Sue Bennett, who might help. Eventually I drifted off to sleep, but the last thing I remembered was Nigel — would he be a help or a hindrance with our adaption of the old shop into something more modern? And then it all faded, and only dreams remained.

The days passed, busy and sunny, and I had a few walks around the town, reminding me of childhood days. Unfortunately, Nigel insisted on accompanying me and talking all the time. He quizzed me about my life in London.

'A boyfriend? Of course you have — still together are you?'

I finally said sharply, 'Look, Nigel, I know you're interested in everything and everybody, but just leave me alone, please. And stop being so fussy with Aunt Cis — all your ideas are confusing her. I suggest you find something else to interest you while you're here, like a new job.' And I hoped he might take the hint not to stay much longer.

But, of course, the main thing he wanted to discuss was the idea of amalgamating antiques and vintage clothes. And he became really helpful, with suggestions about slightly shifting the counter, opening up the back room, painting the walls and lightening it up, and then getting in rails for my clothes. Aunt Cis became very enthusiastic, and as we saw the work progressing, we actually started praising Nigel for his excellent ideas.

And then, one evening, with the shop shut and our supper finished, he asked to look at old family photographs.

'Get a few memories going, Aunt Cis, which I'd like to sort out. I expect you've got lots of old things I could look at.'

She thought for a moment, and then, 'Yes, Nigel, there's a big old suitcase somewhere in the attic full of family things. It would be helpful if you brought it down and looked through all the junk. Plenty of stuff to throw away, I daresay. Yes, lots of things I put away after Denys died . . . '

He went upstairs as we cleared away the dishes and then came down breathless and covered in cobwebs and dust, with a big old tattered suitcase in his arms.

'Look at this! I'll put it in the shop and have a good sort through, shall I? I'll bring you anything interesting and you can tell me about it, Aunt.'

And that was the evening when he discovered a beautiful small swan, tarnished and covered in dust, which I imagined must be an heirloom.

Aunt Cis looked at it in amazement, and then said, almost to herself, 'Goodness, that old thing! We always said it was a lucky charm — and now it's turned up again! One of Denys's favourite pieces, and I hid it away, didn't I, when he went? Well, I'll give it a good clean, and perhaps we'll display it somewhere in the shop. Look, Mel, isn't it lovely?'

I held the small swan in my hand and at once all sorts of thoughts rushed into my mind. This could be a charm for the new boutiques — a new name, perhaps? Something to give us a fresh start and attract new customers; and then another, even more important idea: this little silver heirloom, so important to Aunt Cis, and perhaps to our future, must have a value. And I knew a silversmith, didn't I?

A professional craftsman who would be able to tell us a bit about its past life, and how to deal with it in the new era which I sensed was definitely ahead of it.

I suggested this to Aunt Cis, who agreed, saying, 'Denys always said it was valuable.' And so I carefully took the swan away from Nigel, who seemed inclined to hold on to it, and took it up to bed with me so that he wouldn't try and grab it again.

And yes, tomorrow I would go and find Rick Martin.

4

I looked around the town, searching for Rick Martin, but of course there was no sign of him. But then Allegra Smith came hurrying down the street, stopped, gave me a huge smile, and said, 'Melody! The girl with the lovely name! Hallo, love, and what are you doing today?'

It came out without any hesitation. 'I'm trying to find Rick Martin.'

'Really?' Her keen eyes searched my face. 'He's sharing Gary Miller's workshop — down there by the river, just along from The Anchor Inn. I expect he'll be there, busy working on Mrs Sothern's commission, you know — the bracelet for Charlotte, her daughter . . . '

'Yes,' I said, remembering the commission from the lady of the manor. So he'd got it! 'Thank you, Allegra, I'll go and find him. Cheerio.' And I ran off before she could start in on any more gossip.

It was lovely down there beside the wide, fast-flowing greeny-grey river. There were some boats drawn up on the sandy beach with men busily doing repairs or whatever they do with boats. And I heard faint music — something loud and fast — and grinned to myself. What had Rick said? That Gary's music wasn't for him — so I must be nearly there. I walked on, led by the increasingly brash sound and soon found myself by an open door from which noisy and rhythmic music poured. I ventured in.

It was a workshop, quite obviously, full of tools and mess, and lit with the sunshine drifting in through four large windows. And two men working. The one working at the front of the shed looked at me, and said, 'Can I help you?'

'Yes, please. I'm looking for Rick Martin.' And then I saw him, at the back of the workshop, bent over a big wooden block, with tools and machinery spread around him. He looked so occupied, not raising his eyes as I approached, that for a moment I felt uncomfortable. But then finally, as I halted beside him, he looked up, put down the tool he was holding, and let a warm smile shine out.

'Melody! Just what we haven't got here! Have you come especially with a gentle tune to help soothe my fevered brow?' He was laughing, and I laughed, too, suddenly glad to be here, and hoping Gary would switch off the pop music for a few moments.

'I've come to ask you something, Rick. I want your advice.'

He sat up straighter and stretched his arms above his head. 'Sounds interesting. But let's go outside if we're going to talk.' He got up, gestured me towards the open door, and then, as we walked past Gary's workbench, lent towards him and shouted, 'No need to turn it off, mate. I'll be outside for ten minutes but of course I still want to hear it.'

Gary grinned, and aimed a blow at him, but Rick ducked, and then we were outside, walking towards a bench lower down the riverside. We sat down and smiled at each other. The sun shone through the trees sheltering us, and I thought Rick's blue eyes matched the patches of summer sky high above us.

'Nice to see you again, Mel,' he said after a pause. 'So what's all this about wanting my advice?'

I sat up straighter. After all I was here for a purpose, not just to sit beside Rick and admire the colour of his eyes. Firmly, I said, 'My aunt, Mrs Bartlett, who runs the antique business, has found an old family heirloom, and we think it might have some value. I — well, I just thought you were the person to come and talk to.' I had my bag on my lap now, opening it, and carefully taking out the well-wrapped silver swan. Removing the wrapping I held it — just the right size to fit in my hand — and clean and shining now, after all that wiping and polishing last night. It looked lovely and I hoped Rick would agree. But I wasn't prepared for his reaction. He lent forward, staring down at the swan. 'Surely not — can't be — but it might be . . . ' He was clearly fascinated, so I offered him the bird, and very carefully he took it in both hands, bringing it nearer to his eyes, looking at it as if it was a treasure of some sort.

I hadn't expected this, and said, rather diffidently, 'So what do you think, Rick? Worth anything?'

And then he laughed, very softly, but with mirth filling his face, as he handed me back the swan. 'Worth a few hundred, at least, Mel. And a London valuer might say much more. Where has it come from?'

'Aunt Cis said it was a childhood lucky charm.' I felt rather silly, not knowing quite what to say after his amazing revelation. In order to cover up my confusion, I wrapped up the swan again, and put it safely back in my bag. I looked at Rick and saw he was clearly trying to sort out his thoughts. 'Tell me,' I said quietly, 'tell me what this is all about.'

'Well . . . ' He leaned back against the bench and I met his eyes; a startling colour in the sunshine. They looked at me with an expression which I felt uncomfortable with, as he asked, 'Where did your aunt get it from?'

I said quickly, 'Are you suggesting she stole it, or something?'

And then he laughed, and the expression became softer, and very amused. 'Not you or your aunt, Mel. I don't see either of you as thieves at all, but this, if I'm right, it could well be something quite valuable.' He was looking at me very intently, and I thought how lucky we were to have someone like him to go to for advice. Did he read my thoughts?

He asked, 'Want me to find out about it, Mel? I've got books, internet, all sorts of stuff I could research.'

I said at once, 'Yes, please, Rick. We do want to know as much as possible about it. You see . . . ' I hesitated, but his expression was full of interest, so I went on. 'Aunt and I have the idea of using this little swan as a sort of logo — something to catch the public eye when we open our new boutiques.'

'New boutiques? Sounds good. Where are you planning to move to?'

I laughed, feeling a bit embarrassed. 'Not moving anywhere! But expanding the antique shop to make two smaller — more modern — boutiques. Aunt Cis is all for it, and so am I. You see, Nigel's idea sounded ridiculous at first, but then, when we thought about it, we saw the sense of what he was suggesting.'

Rick was silent for a moment, then, 'Who's this Nigel? Your boyfriend?'

I saw the gleam in his eyes and was confused for a second. But I said very quickly, 'No, he's a distant cousin of some sort. Staying while he looks for a new job.' I stopped, because the expression on his face made me wonder what he was thinking. Then I said, sharply, and with an edge to my voice, 'I don't have a boyfriend. Not at the moment. So it's good to think about a new career.'

He nodded slowly, but didn't take his eyes off me. 'And what's the new career to be?'

'Vintage clothes.' And I was glad to be on a safer subject. 'I'm taking over the back part of Aunt Cis's shop front, there's room for both of us. And I thought a logo like Silver Swan Crafts would be very appealing. So that's why we want to know . . . '

'Of course. Very practical. I'll find out what I can for you. And now I must get back to work.' We walked back to the workshop and stopped at the open doorway. Loud music was still wafting out. We smiled at each other. Rick nodded towards the bag I carried, and said, 'Look after it, Mel. Could be a valuable object. I'll let you know when I've found out a bit of its history. Nice to have seen you — cheers for now.' And he went into the workshop.

I walked slowly back to the town centre, loath to leave the river and the thought of that companionable little time sitting with him among the trees and the sunshine. Then I told myself not to be so foolish, and went back to find Aunt Cis and tell her my news about the swan. Nigel was working in the small back room and came into the main shop as I said that Rick would research it. He put down his tape measure, stuck a pencil behind his ear and perched on the counter.

'Can you trust him, this Rick Martin?' he asked. 'Got to be careful, you know, Mel — don't want to let anyone crooked get hold of the thing, do we?'

I turned and gave him a freezing stare. 'Rick is a respectable craftsman. He's certainly not crooked.' Then I said to Aunt Cis, 'I'm going to find Sue Bennett this afternoon and ask her about finding new stock. And I must contact Lissa, too — there's a lot to do.' I certainly didn't want to sit there and listen to Nigel fantasizing about honest people making a bid to steal our silver swan.

Good to have plenty to think about, I told myself, going up to my room and computer where I could email Lissa in London. But as I went upstairs, Nigel's words rang in my head. 'Can you trust him, this Rick Martin?' he'd asked and now, as I sat down at the computer and tried to put words together to send Lissa a message, the answer rang through me.

Yes, I knew I could trust Rick. The truth hit me like a rock, and I smiled as if I had suddenly found a jewel in the dust and litter of our work downstairs. The words to Lissa came easily now, and I knew my morning errand had given me just what I needed to help settle into my upside-down life. I found Sue Bennett in her little shop in the market square. It was a small space, with little light, but she had arranged some attractive clothes all around and there were shelves full of shoes, hats, gloves and scarves.

She greeted me warmly. 'Well, hiya, Mel. I was wondering if I should see you. Come to a decision, have you, about starting your business again?' She pulled a chair out beside her at the small counter and I sat down, looking around at the variety of clothes. I realized that she showed off the ordinary second hand clothes on a Friday when her stall was in the market, but here was the core of her vintage business.

I said, 'Yes, I have, Sue. Aunt Cis and I are forming her old shop into a couple of modern boutiques, and so I must start stocking up. I've come to see if you have any more lovely old things.'

She nodded, and smiled. 'You're welcome to look around. I'll ask a fair price so that you can get a good start. I expect you'll want to get together a variety of things — there's a really smart '50s wedding hat, over there, all feathers — and what about that 1930s sundress? And look in that cupboard at the back — I keep gloves and underwear there.' She grinned. 'And how about a Victorian nightdress?'

A customer arrived then, so I got up and whispered to her, 'I'll look around,' and slipped away from the counter. Half an hour later, with the customer disappearing from the shop, I put my choices in front of Sue and said, 'I'd like these four things, please. Can you spare them? And what'll you charge me?' I waited anxiously. My savings weren't very big but I needed some good stock to fill the new little shop.

Sue looked through the pieces — the feather hat, the sundress, a Victorian camisole, and some satin dancing shoes that must have trodden a good few measures, for they were scuffed at the toes, and I could imagine the wearer smiling up at her partner as they danced through the night. Carefully she put them all in a big, elegant paper bag and slid them across the counter towards me, saying, 'Take them, love, and I'll charge you payment at the end of the month. That'll give you a chance to get cracking.'

I was so surprised that I couldn't find words for a minute, but finally I stuttered, 'Sue, that's so good of you, but are you quite sure you can wait that long?'

Her smile was warm, and lit up her face. 'Mel, I have a feeling we can be friends, and I'd like that so much. Yes, of course, it's all right. I know you're honest, and I wish you well with the new venture.' She paused, then she added, 'And perhaps you'll come round for supper one evening? I feel we've got a lot to talk about, vintage clothes, and perhaps families and so on.'

I nodded, suddenly touched by her soft voice and warmth of feeling. A new friend. And if I was going to settle here in Stretton, this was just what I needed. Someone a little older, more experienced I felt, who could advise me and listen to my complaints about Nigel, and worries about Aunt Cis.

I left the little shop carrying the big bag and already planning just how to display the gorgeous vintage clothes I had acquired. I smiled as I walked back to the antique shop, telling myself that Silver Swan Crafts was taking the first step into its future.

5

Aunt Cis was delighted with my new purchases, and we spent some time examining them, and then planning the layout of the small back room, now slightly bigger and altogether much more attractive.

She said, 'Nigel's gone out to buy some spotlights. He says they'll really light up the space so that your clothes can be seen properly. You know, Mel, I think he's doing a good job, after all — not quite so hopeless as he seemed at first! Perhaps we should be kinder to him, what do you think?'

I smoothed out the Victorian nightdress and decided to give it a good airing and pressing before hanging it somewhere. 'I suppose so — yes, he's been quite helpful so far. And spotlights will definitely be good, giving a rather subtle light to the clothes.' I smiled at her, and then added, 'But I don't want to encourage him to take too big a part in the new business, Aunt. I think he could be tricky if he wanted to. Do you know what I mean?'

She nodded slowly. 'Always a young man who did whatever he wanted, was Nigel. Oh, and here he is now . . . '

He came rushing in, putting a pile of hefty boxes on the small table that I was putting my clothes on.

'Careful!' I exclaimed. 'They're quite thin and delicate — don't push them about like that.'

He looked at me with a frown and muttered something about couldn't I be more grateful, and then tore open the boxes, revealing the spotlights and examining them.

I was irritated by his lack of thought. 'Nigel, these are very old garments, and I don't want them messed about. Please don't handle them.'

For a moment I saw anger on his face. 'About time you showed a bit of gratitude, Mel, I should say,' he muttered, and then took the spotlights into the kitchen. I met Aunt Cis's frown, and knew I must mend my ways with difficult Nigel. I lay down the clothes very carefully, and followed him to the kitchen table, where he was sorting out the spotlights into various small groups.

'Sorry, Nigel,' I said, finding a small smile and turning it on him. 'Don't mean to be unkind, but I'm used to running my business without much help, so please forgive me if I get a bit hasty. And yes, you really are being helpful.'

He put down the last spotlight, stared at me, and then slowly smiled, coming back into the kitchen entrance and putting an arm on my shoulder. 'Nothing to worry about, Mel,' he said gently. 'I guess you're having problems about the boyfriend leaving, aren't you? Can't be easy being on your own again. You know, a woman alone . . . So let's kiss and make up, shall we?' His smile grew, and he bent and kissed my cheek before dropping his arm and going back to the spotlight plan.

To say I was surprised was the least of it. Nigel, kissing me! What on earth should I do? I just stood there, one hand to my cheek which he had just kissed, and stared at him. Things were moving, I thought — but was this the direction I wanted them to go in?

That afternoon Nigel said he had something important to do, so he disappeared, leaving Aunt Cis and me looking at each other with puzzled faces. 'What on earth?' I said as I returned to my heap of vintage clothes, and put ready the ironing board to give them all a good press. 'He's such a complete idiot — I thought he was going to deal with the spotlights, but now he's gone off somewhere. He's really unreliable.' I switched on the iron and picked up the sundress, looking very carefully at it for any tagged seams or stray bits of cotton thread.

Aunt Cis sat down at her counter and produced her knitting. Clearly it was going to be a restful afternoon. She smiled at me, and said quietly, 'I hope you're going to tell me about going to this young man — this silversmith you've found. What did he say when he saw the swan?'

I tested the iron and found it not hot enough yet. I said slowly, 'He was impressed, actually. Didn't say much, except that it could be, or it might be, which wasn't much help.'

Aunt Cis laid down her knitting again. 'Could be? Might be what? Something valuable, do you suppose?'

I shook my head. 'Don't think so. He didn't say, but he's going to do some research and then let me — us — know.'

She was watching me very closely, and I felt myself start to colour under her gaze. I knew how keenly Aunt Cis could look at one, and how she was able to sort out one's emotions and secrets. I cleared my throat, said huskily, 'He's very busy, got a big commission on, apparently. So not much time to spare.'

The knitting needles were clacking

again. 'In that case, good of him to show an interest,' said Aunt Cis. 'I expect he'll take his time.'

I ironed the creased bodice of the orange sundress and looked particularly at the small brown flowers decorating it. Concentrate on your new business and don't fuss about Rick Martin. But Aunt Cis was on the job and not giving it up. 'So what's he like, this young man of yours?' she asked.

My young man! Now my cheeks were really getting warm. I didn't look at her. 'Oh, quite nice. Ordinary. You know.'

She tried again. 'No, I don't. That's why I'm asking, Mel. I feel we must know a bit more about him if he's going to help us with our silver swan. And you've got it safe, haven't you?'

'Upstairs in my dressing table drawer, wrapped up and well hidden.' I moved the sundress so that the skirt lay on the ironing board. I changed the subject. 'This is very good cotton, quite nice quality, I should get a good price for it . . .'

'I'm waiting for a description of this young man,' said Aunt Cis in a steely voice that I recalled from naughty adolescent years. I looked up, caught her eye, and we both laughed. 'All right,' I said, 'if you really have to know.'

'And I do, if you please, Mel.'

'Well, he's tall, about six foot one or two I should think. Good shoulders, and very slim, but large hands.' I put down the iron, and looked into a scene Aunt Cis couldn't see. The river bank, with blue patches of sky, and Rick's eyes smiling at me . . . For a second I lingered there, until I smelt hot iron, and then I was back in the half-finished new boutique, working at my new business. 'He's not bad-looking, his hair is untidy, long and very dark, as are his eyebrows, his eyes are the palest blue, and his voice is fabulously dark and low,' I said quickly, and returned to the ironing.

There was a moment's quietness, and then the needles started clacking again, and Aunt Cis said, in her amused, elderly voice, 'Well, thank you Mel, for such a good description. I can almost see Rick Martin — he sounds like a proper craftsman, and I look forward to meeting him.'

And, as I progressed with the ironing, I told myself that I was also looking forward to our next meeting. And if he didn't come and call on us here in the shop, then I would definitely go down to the river workshop again. I smiled as I ironed the other side of the sundress skirt.

Nigel was out for most of the afternoon and we were getting slightly worried about him. Where could he have gone? And without telling us? I had a bit of a bad thought that perhaps all the hard work in the shop had been too much for him and that he'd decided to do a runner without telling us. Surely not! He'd been so keen about the spotlights, and setting up my new counter in the little room — and even shown an interest in the clothes I had been sorting out.

I said, 'Do you think he's just gone off? You know, easy come, easy go? Well, that's the way he arrived, isn't it? I mean, what ought we to do?'

She got up from the counter and headed for the kitchen. 'Those are very defeatist thoughts, Mel,' she said over her shoulder, her voice quite sharp for once, 'and don't become you. Of course Nigel will come back. As I keep telling you, the boy is family.'

'But — ' I began, all to no avail.

Another glance over her shoulder, and steely eyes, and, 'He will return. When did Nigel ever willingly miss his cup of tea and piece of flapjack?'

I shook my head, even as I thought of muggings and kidnappings, but knew I must go along with wise Aunt Cis. And then I wondered about contacting that all-knowledgeable Allegra Smith — she would know, surely, if anything had happened to Nigel? But what a fuss to make in the town, and I knew Aunt Cis would never forgive me for raising the hue and cry if not necessary. And of course Nigel was a strong man and would be able to fight down any attacker . . . I switched off the iron and told myself I was being a fool. Attacker? Don't be ridiculous, Mel. Stretton was a quiet, community minded little town. No baddies here, not like London. And anyway, any minute and he'd be here. And why was I so worried about him? Surely it couldn't be that I had a fondness for distant cousin Nigel?

And thank goodness, that made me laugh. Out loud, so that Aunt Cis, poking her head around the open doorway, said, 'And what's that all about? Has he come back?'

I was about to stop my chuckling and say no, when we both heard the back door open. We looked down the passage and saw Nigel — hurray, he's safe, I thought — coming in with a huge smile on his face.

He came up to Aunt Cis, grinned even more at her, and said, 'I've brought someone to see you, darling Aunt Cis. A surprise visit.'

I watched her face tighten for a moment, but then open out into a welcome expression. 'How nice, Nigel,' she said. 'And must you keep whoever it is standing out in the stable yard? Better invite him — her — in, hadn't you?' She turned back into the kitchen. 'I'll just put out another cup.'

Nigel disappeared out through the doorway again, and I stood there, wondering who the visitor might be. I didn't have to wonder very long. He came back clutching something very carefully, something which looked like a body, and which almost covered him as he trundled it along the passage towards me. 'This is Dolly,' he said with a great grin. 'She's going to model your old clothes for you, Mel. I do hope you're pleased?'

6

I was speechless, just standing there, staring at Dolly's pale unclothed body, her pale, unpainted face, her lack of hair. And yet — there was definitely something about the dressmaker's dummy that spoke to me. Even though no voice came, I thought I heard one: please dress me up to look pretty and I will sell some of your precious old clothes. And then I said, in a rush, with great warmth and joy in my voice, 'Nigel! You really are wonderful! Oh, thank you so much — I must give you a kiss, I'm so grateful!' And there I was, hugging the poor chap even as he stood there with Dolly leaning against him. They both nearly fell over, but I managed to help him keep his balance. 'Where did you get it — I mean her?'

'Saw an ad in the local paper, so took the van.'

'Took my van?' Aunt Cis was cross.

He gave her a huge smile, put down Dolly on her wooden stand, and crossed the room, hugging Aunt as he reached her. 'I only borrowed it for half an hour. I knew you wouldn't want me to take it, but — well, I just did.'

How could we be cross with him? I continued to look at Dolly, seeing in my mind's eye all those lovely vintage clothes hanging so elegantly around her smooth body. 'I shall put the nightgown on first,' I said, 'and just see what she looks like. Perhaps a little linen cap on her hair.'

'But she hasn't got any hair,' said Aunt Cis, narrowing her eyes and staring at the dummy. 'Do you know, I think we might just give her some eyes — shall I get my paintbox? Blue or brown, do you think?' And she disappeared out of the shop.

'Well, Nigel, we're very grateful to you,' I said, trying to make amends for my hugging him. 'And do you think you could get on with the spotlights now? You see — ' I stopped, for the bell on the door jangled and I knew I must keep out of the way of Aunt's customers. But it wasn't a customer who came in, it was Allegra Smith, complete with clipboard, and tearing papers off as she entered. I said, 'Good afternoon, Miss Smith.'

At once she came up to me and said rapidly, 'I have entries for the Craft Competititon — Mel, isn't it? Yes, I remember you. That lovely name. And I hear that you and Mrs Bartlett are opening up this old shop.' A bit of an apologetic smile, here. 'Well, I don't mean to be rude, but of course, it is old — but that it's going to become new and very elegant. Is that so? I don't usually get my facts wrong.'

My mouth had fallen open, but now I quickly closed it. I said, 'Yes, you're right, Miss Smith, but I can't imagine where you heard all this. We haven't told many people so far.'

'So it's good that I'm here. And do call me Allegra, my dear. For of course you'll need marketing and lots of PR, won't you? And I'm the person to give it you. May I have a look around? Ah yes, I see, this is a small room that you are converting into a subtle gown shop, while your aunt maintains her counter table and the spaces all around her. Should work well. When do you open?'

I was breathless with all this, and by now Aunt Cis had returned with her paintbox and stood in the doorway, wide-eyed. I said, 'I expect you know Allegra, Aunt Cis,' hoping that she did.

Without a pause Allegra nodded to her and said, 'Oh yes, old friends, Mrs Bartlett and me. Now, Mel, when is the opening date, if you please?'

I was quite relieved when Nigel politely pushed in front of me, and smiled at the maddening woman with her clipboard and pile of entry forms. 'A fortnight tomorrow,' he said and I thought, he's just saying the first date in his mind. 'We shall be ready for the public then, Allegra, and perhaps you will be good enough to give us a little boost — say ten a.m.? Mel and I and Aunt Cis will all be here, dressed in our very best, and waiting for customers. I should say clients.' He grinned. 'Sounds so much more elegant, don't you think?'

Allegra stood her ground, waving forms at him, and finally answering, 'Sounds good, Nigel. What is this new craft shop to be called? Something in keeping with the new look, I hope? There are some very strange names around already in the town.'

I heard the name vibrating in my head, and met her keen eyes with a ready smile. 'Yes, it's to be called Silver Swan Crafts. And thank you for agreeing to publicize us, Allegra. But now we really must get on with the work — if you don't mind . . . '

Just for a few seconds there was silence; she said nothing, but dropped her jaw in astonishment that anyone should order her about, and then Nigel took her arm and led her to the door, smiling, and said, in a very pleasant way,

'So kind of you to come, Allegra. And we'll see you again very soon. Goodbye, for now . . . '

Aunt Cis and I stood in the dusty space between door and counter, and watched the vanquishment of Allegra Smith. Yes, she went, but even as she walked up the hill, she waved back at us and smiled her enormous smile of self-satisfaction.

Nigel turned to me. 'Tea?' he asked, and obediently I went to the kitchen and put the kettle on. I felt needed some fresh air after we had a cup of reviving tea, so took myself off down to the river, telling Aunt Cis I would probably drop in on Rick Martin and see if he had any news of the swan. I was nearing the workshop when I saw a girl standing in the open doorway, talking to someone and smiling as she did so.

For a moment I paused. I hadn't thought that Rick might have a girlfriend, so I stood under the trees, undecided as to what I should do next.

But the girl chose that moment to turn around, saw me, and then turned back and I heard her say, 'Are you expecting someone? A tall girl with chestnut hair . . .'

And almost at once Rick appeared in the doorway. He waved at me to come nearer, which I did, and then he introduced me to the waiting girl. 'Mel, this is Charlotte Sothern. Charlie, this is Mel.'

We looked at each other, and I felt instantly that she had taken a dislike to me. Ridiculous, perhaps, but there it was. I smiled and said, 'I was just calling to see if you had any news, Rick, but if you're busy I'll come another day,' and Charlie butted in.

'I was just going. But make sure the bracelet is ready for Friday, won't you, Rick? Mother's set her heart on having it by then. Oh, and don't forget, you're invited to the party. Do come?' She put a hand on his arm and gave him a big smile.

Rick just nodded and said, 'Thanks, Charlie. Yes, I'd love to come.' He turned to me, raised a dark, thick eyebrow, waited for me to nod an unthinking yes please, and he then looked back at Charlie. 'I'll bring a friend,' he said.

'Oh,' she said, clearly not pleased. 'Well, yes, of course, if you want to . . . '

We looked at each other for a long moment, and then she turned and walked very fast towards the town, and disappeared from view.

I looked at Rick. His smile was full of amusement, but, 'Women!' was all he said. Then he looked back into the workshop. 'Going off now, Gary — I deserve an early night, and I've got someone who wants to talk to me. See you tomorrow.'

He took my hand and led me to the bench where we had sat before, and I didn't say a thing, just went with him. He sat back, and looked at me with those keen, pale eyes. 'You want to know if I found anything out about your swan? Well, not much, which will disappoint you, I'm sure. But I have a contact in London who knows about these old forgotten things that sometimes turn up in kitchens and attics. Or even at boot sales. And I wondered — ' He turned and looked at me very straight. 'It's a lot to ask, Mel, but would you let me borrow the swan and take it up to this guy? I could do it in a day or a day and a half.'

My mind was full of awkward thoughts. What about his work? The bracelet for Charlotte's birthday on Friday? Would he have finished it? Was it fair to ask him to go? And then, a warm glow to think that he was keen to do so — for me. I found myself very confused. Asking him to give up his time was one thing, and of course it was amazing that he would do so, but what about my fear of having to trust a man again? And to trust this particular man with such an important — could be valuable — object as the famous silver swan.

I didn't answer at once — how could I? I was so unsure about everything.

Slowly he reached out and took my hand. 'Got a problem with letting me have it, Mel? I understand if you have, and in that case I'll send a sketch of the swan to this guy in London. But it would only be for a day, you know.' His strong fingers encased my hand and I felt his warmth entering me, and, along with that warmth a sensible question which only I could answer — could I trust this man to take the swan and then bring it back again?

He was smiling at me, clearly amused because of my caution. 'Honestly, Mel, I haven't got a police record or anything and I'd like you to know you can trust me. In fact, I'll leave my notebook with you as an assurance that I'll be back. Will that do?'

And then, of course, I could only smile shamefacedly and mutter, 'Of course it will. But you don't really need to . . .'

'It's settled. Here's the notebook. I'll come with you and collect the swan and I'll catch the early morning train.' He pulled the notebook out of his pocket and put it on my lap. He watched me put it in my own pocket, then said casually, 'And now how about going into The Anchor on the way and having a celebratory drink?'

I got up and blinked at him. 'Celebratory, Rick?'

He grinned as we walked towards the pub. 'I'm getting the swan, you've got my notebook. Got to be a celebration in there somewhere. Come on, Mel, I'm thirsty after a day's work.'

We had our drink, sitting outside the busy pub, and beginning to get to know a bit about each other, and then I took him to the shop where Aunt Cis had already shut up the shutters and locked the door, but let us in to the kitchen. I introduced them and I saw Aunt Cis run her sharp eyes over Rick's long hair and shabby jacket and for a moment I wondered if I was being foolish to trust him. But then who should come into the kitchen but Nigel, who had fiddled with the spotlights for what seemed hours and still hadn't got them installed.

'Damn things,' he snorted, as he came through the doorway and then stopped, staring at Rick. 'And who are you? Know anything about putting in spotlights, do you? I've been trying, but something seems to fall apart all the time.'

Rick looked at him, then at the light in his hand. 'I had a job putting in mine, but I managed it. Let me see — have you got the connection firm enough? Like this . . . '

He stood on a chair inside my little room, fixing something to the wall, and then, there was the light, beaming down on Dolly, and making everything look rather glamorous and different.

Nigel pulled a face. 'I don't see how — '

'Like this.'

Two pairs of hands fiddled with the rest of the spotlights, and I decided I'd seen enough. Rick must have the swan. I whispered to Aunt Cis, 'Can you trust him with the swan, if we have his notebook?'

Without a pause she said a definite, 'Yes. I think he's all right — but I'll have a look at the notebook, it could be interesting.' Then she smiled at us all and said, 'While you're upstairs, Mel, I'll make us a nice pot of coffee. And there are some new flapjacks . . . I expect you've got a sweet tooth, Rick, haven't you?'

As I ran upstairs, I heard him say, 'Yes, but how did you know?' and wanted to laugh, because Aunt Cis seemed to know just the right thing to say at the right moment.

7

I awoke very early next morning and at once thought about Rick catching the early train to London. In his pocket, well wrapped, would be our silver swan. I didn't allow any more doubts to trouble me; somehow I trusted him because he'd been so willing to leave his notebook, and that was an essential part of his work. I didn't see how he would carry off our swan and then return to his work without the return of his famous notebook. And, as Aunt Cis had said, it would be interesting to look at his entries in the book. I found myself being more and more interested in him, and not just as a craftsman, but as a person. The sort of man I hadn't met for many a long year, I thought dreamily — but then I jumped out of bed, told myself to stop this nonsense and get on with the important work of setting up Silver Swan

Crafts. Nigel had told Allegra it would open on Friday fortnight — and that gave us just ten more days to get cracking with the final touches. I hurried down to breakfast and was delighted to find a large parcel from London delivered — vintage clothes from Lissa. I could hardly wait to open it and when I did, I was so grateful to my ex-partner — for she had sent me some really lovely clothes, with a little note which simply said, 'Good luck, and hope these fly out the door! Love, Lissa.'

I felt quietly emotional, thinking of how hard we had worked in London, and how sad it had been to forget Tony, and say goodbye and catch a train down here to quiet, dull Devon. Then I looked at Dolly, standing by the window in my new little boutique, and realized just how wrong my expectations had been. Quiet? Dull? Not with Allegra ordering us about; Nigel and his surreal ideas; and finally, dear Aunt Cis wielding her paintbox and giving Dolly a most glamorous, elegant expression, with greeny-blue eyes downcast, and apparently showing her most naive qualities. For suddenly the plain dummy had become a simple girl with a fetching, shy smile, and long eyelashes that outdid any I had ever seen on a makeup counter.

'Aunt Cis,' I said joyfully, 'you've surpassed yourself. Dolly looks marvellous! How clever of you — and look, Lissa has sent this gorgeous Edwardian hat — all it needs is a squashy white rose and Dolly can wear it with this long floaty black skirt and my Devore jacket — just the thing to start us off on Friday week, don't you think?'

Aunt Cis started piling up the breakfast dishes and said, over her shoulder, 'I'm glad you're pleased. I did the eyes last night before you came in with Rick. And I thought we might just find a moment to look at his notebook before I open the shop this morning?'

I stopped unfolding all Lissa's clothes, and thought for a bit. Rick would almost certainly be in London by now, and so it was right for Aunt and me to look at his notebook — I was curious to know what his work was like. In a way I was curious, but almost afraid that he might not be as talented as I imagined him to be. If I didn't like his work, would it make me feel differently about him as a person? And then I followed Aunt out to the kitchen to help with the washing up, telling myself very sensibly that I had no feelings about Rick Martin at all, except that he was being very helpful over the matter of the swan.

And then Nigel came striding into the kitchen, arms full of flowers and foliage. He plonked it all down on the table, grinned at me and said, 'There you are, plenty of stuff for you to fiddle around with and make the place look pretty. I got it cheap from the grocery shop in town — stuff they can't sell, but which looks fairly good still.'

I picked up a single stem of a hideous dying pink daisy, and said, 'Thanks, Nigel. What a load of dead old stuff — I can't imagine what you think I can do with this.'

But Aunt Cis turned from the sink, looked at the muddle of half-dead flowers, and said quietly, 'We can keep the bits that are still green, and I'll make an arrangement of leaves and twigs which will give a nice rural feel to the room. Put them aside, Mel, and I'll deal with them later. For the moment they can go in water and recover a bit . . . '

Nigel came to my side when I returned to the small room and continued sorting out Lissa's clothes.

'So who was that guy here last night, Mel? Your latest boyfriend, was he? A scruffy-looking chap, if you ask me.'

'But I didn't ask you, Nigel, as I recall. That was Rick Martin, the town silversmith, who is doing us a very good favour by taking the swan up to London . . . '

'WHAT?' Nigel's roar took me by surprise. 'Don't tell me you gave him the swan? And he's gone off to London with it? Are you raving mad, Mel? The man's probably on his way out of the country this very minute. Honestly, how could you be so stupid?'

I felt my anger ignite and start to burn but I kept my temper. 'Nigel, you don't understand anything. Rick has gone to show the swan to a contact who knows about such things, and will be back again early tomorrow morning. With the swan.'

He pulled a face. 'That's what you think. I bet he doesn't come back and then that's that — the swan gone, no hopes of finding out its value, and the end of these two new boutiques.'

Aunt Cis coughed slightly, and made us look at her. She remained impassive, but I saw the light in her eyes and knew we were misbehaving. 'I'm going to open the shop,' she said, 'and I would be grateful if any further arguments you two intend to have could continue in the kitchen, or even outside in the stable yard. All this unpleasantness is not good for trade, thank you very much.'

I felt the charged atmosphere suddenly lessen, and looked at Nigel. He, too, seemed caught out. We both nodded at each other, and I said quietly, 'Sorry, Aunt Cis. We really shouldn't explode like that — but Nigel must realize that Rick is to be trusted. Can you persuade him to do so, do you think?'

'I should be pleased to look at Rick's notebook with Nigel — perhaps there he will see the sort of man who is doing this for us. Now, Nigel, come and look at this . . . '

I left them in the front of the shop, opening the notebook and silently sitting behind the counter, looking at it. Meanwhile I got out the iron, and started a big programme of pressing slightly creased vintage clothes. And while I ironed I thought of Rick, meeting his contact, and wondered what, if anything, he was finding out.

Once the ironing was done, I went out into the town, with a few errands to do, but mostly because I wanted to call on Sue Bennett and ask if she had any spare scarves which I could add to a few of my own and some that Aunt Cis had dug out of a forgotten drawer. She had also given me a rather dilapidated old spice box which still smelt evocative and which I thought would make a good lucky dip tub for the scarves. And then there was the lovely mellow walnut jewellery box which she had said I could show on my table, with some very glittery stones and beads falling out of it. I aimed for a glamorous, but subtle sort of display which would hint at quality and elegance as well as colour and rich texture. As the days went by I was becoming more and more excited at the thought of opening Silver Swan Crafts, and found great satisfaction in setting up my small boutique.

After doing all the errands on my list I headed for Sue's shop. She was sitting behind her counter immersed in some crochet, which she put down at once as I entered. 'Mel — how nice to see you. I was wondering how you were getting on down there in the antiques department!'

I returned her warm smile. 'It's all

coming along splendidly, Sue — and we're opening on Friday week! Allegra's been in and cased the joint and is giving us some PR. And we've filled in the forms for entry into the Craft Award — just to keep her quiet, really. I'm sure there are plenty of really talented small businesses in the town which will get ahead of us.' And at once my thoughts ran to Rick — was he on the way home yet? I wondered.

I told Sue about Nigel bringing Dolly, which was a bit of a joke, but who, as I now realized, was the making of the little boutique. 'And I'm in the market for any spare scarves which you might want to get rid of.' Yes, she said, and at once found a box half full of really colourful and nice quality silk scarves.

'Thank you,' I said, and we haggled over a price.

'So — ' She looked at me very keenly. 'Everything going OK? No problems?'

I told her about the silver swan, and I could see she was enchanted with the idea of it. 'I haven't got it at the moment, though,' I said bleakly, 'and I'm hoping Rick Martin will bring it back this evening.'

She hesitated, and then asked, 'You sound as if you're not sure about him. All I know is that he's a terrific silversmith, and a nice guy. Are you worried? I don't think you should be.'

I heaved a big sigh for suddenly it seemed my mind was full of worries. Nigel, Aunt Cis finding the business too much for her, Rick taking the swan . . . I said slowly, 'Life's a bit complicated, Sue.'

'When isn't it? All you can do is take it as it comes, and hope for the best.' Her smile was full of experience, and then she added, 'I've had my share of problems, Mel, but believe me, we all get through them. So don't worry about the tricky men in your life — or your aunt, for I'm sure she's as strong as an ox beneath all that seeming old age. And having you here must be wonderful for her. Don't worry. Just live. It'll all be fine.'

And I believed her. I went back to the shop carrying the scarves and full of new thoughts. Rick would bring back the swan, of course he would. Aunt Cis would live to a vast old age. Nigel would find a job — one day. And I would develop my little boutique into a fine new shop with customers coming from all over the county.

It was tea time when I returned to the shop. Aunt Cis had told Nigel to brew a pot and bring out the biscuit tin, and she was carrying on a very lively conversation with an American tourist who wanted hunting prints, and needed to have them explained to him. Aunt Cis seemed in her element, so I quietly took Rick's notebook from the drawer behind the counter and took it off to my little boutique to look at it alone, away from Nigel's chatty conversations, and to be able to really look and think about what the pages showed me.

I had no idea that a craftsman needed to make sketches of what he was hoping to make. But here were all the rough outlines of Rick's works. Neat pencil sketches of candlesticks, dining spoons, pendants, bracelets — this one was near the end of the book so I guessed it was what he was making for Charlotte's birthday, a slender elegant piece of silver chain decorated with stones — lapis lazuli, said his notes, and citrines — with me guessing at the brightness of the blue and crystal depths, and a tiny linking lock that held her initials CS. I let out my breath in a big whoosh — what wonderful workmanship, what delicacy and beauty.

Yes, Rick Martin was indeed a super craftsman. And then, just as I was closing the book, the last page flipped open and there was the sketch of a woman's face, very minute, but with clear features. And they were recognizable. I looked closer, frowned, and then put down the book. Rick Martin had drawn a very faint sketch of me in his work notebook and strange emotions were rising inside me. What could it mean? And what did I feel about it?

But then Nigel came into the room with a mug of tea which he slopped over the floor and made me exclaim with annoyance.

'Sorry,' he said. 'Oh, looking at Martin's book, were you? Yes, a bit arty, but Aunt Cis and I thought he did good work. Now, want a flapjack or a biscuit? Come on, make up your mind — I can't stay here all the afternoon, you know, there's a lot waiting to be done.'

I took a flapjack, wiped my soiled mug, and remembered what Sue had said. Just live. Yes, that's what I would do; extraordinary notebook, Nigel's crass behaviour, Rick returning this evening with the swan. Everything. Just live, Mel, and enjoy your life. And the more I thought about it, the better things became.

8

I thought the next day would never end. I wanted to see Rick return, needed to have the silver swan back again, safely hidden in my drawer upstairs, and somehow the hours dragged. Oh yes, I worked as usual, sorting out my lovely clothes, arranging them on rails, dressing up Dolly, trying on new things, testing the spotlights and fragrant candles, and finally coming to the conclusion that the new boutique was as good as we could make it.

But there at the edge of my busy mind was a feeling of anxiety, tight and uneasy; would Rick return? Or was Nigel right when he suggested the swan might disappear, and Rick with it? I know I was irritable because of this nasty feeling; I snapped at Nigel who then went off in a buzz of quick anger, and set Aunt Cis looking at me with her sharp eyes, and, I felt, blaming me for everything that went wrong during the day. In fact, I was so exhausted by mid-afternoon that I slumped down behind my pretty decorated little table, and pushed aside a basket of gemstones, to make room for a big mug of coffee. I needed some extra energy — I looked at Aunt Cis who was polishing a new set of little cabinets which she had just bought, and said wearily, 'I'm sorry, Aunt, I'm not at my best today.'

She turned, gave me a long look and then bent to her polishing again. 'I would have thought you were old enough to deal with your worries, Mel, my dear. I suppose it's the business of the swan, isn't it? And that handsome young man. Such a storm in a teacup.'

I didn't think that was fair. And said so. 'Aunt Cis, the swan could be extremely valuable — I'm just a bit worried that it might have gone adrift somehow . . . '

'And Rick Martin with it? Yes, I imagined that was part of your worry.'

'Nonsense,' I said quickly. 'Nothing to do with him, it's just the swan that sticks in my mind. I mean, just supposing — not that it'll happen, of course — but imagine, if he DID run off with it, and it was really valuable, then . . . ' I stopped sharp because of her expression. I was a child again, being told off for silly thoughts. I gulped a big mouthful of coffee and felt stronger. 'Well, all right, I won't go on about it. He'll be here this evening, I expect, and then I shall feel better.'

'I sincerely hope so. I miss your usual happy-go-lucky expression. Try and cheer up, my dear.'

I went for a walk when the shop shut. Fresh air, I thought, a glimpse of the shining river, some country sounds, and I'd feel fine again. And ready for Rick's return later in the evening. But Nigel found me there by the bench where Rick and I had sat, and now sat beside me, looking at me with a very worried expression, and hands that kept reaching out to hold mine.

'Mel, I know you've had a difficult day, and I don't want you to feel bad because you shouted at me. I mean, we're cousins — well, distant ones — but we're family, and that's what so important. You see, I understand how you must feel, letting that guy go off with the family heirloom. Yes, of course, you meant well, but perhaps it was just a bit silly, don't you think? Irresponsible, perhaps? After all, you know next to nothing about him, do you?'

I couldn't stand any more of this moralizing, with Nigel's hands stroking mine and my mind getting more and more furious as the minutes passed. I leapt to my feet. 'Leave me alone,' I stormed. 'Just leave me alone! You know nothing at all about Rick, and I wish you'd find a new job and go and do it!'

I left him sitting on the bench, his jaw dropping, and his face showing exactly what he thought of my cousinly affection. I walked very fast away from the river, into the town, and along the road leading to the station. I had no idea when the next London train would arrive, but anything was better than listening to Nigel and sitting alone feeling sorry for myself. I walked the platform several times, discovered that a train was due in ten minutes and then impatiently waited for it to arrive. It came with all the noise and disturbance of modern transport and I stood by the station stairs, watching for passengers to alight.

And there he was. Rick Martin, rucksack on his shoulder, striding along and then seeing me waiting there. He came up to me, narrowed his keen, pale eyes, smiled and said quietly, 'How nice to have a reception committee; good to see you, Mel.' That deep, vibrant voice . . .

I felt that the day had suddenly become wonderful, but I lowered my eyes and said quickly, 'Well, I was just passing, and thought I'd wait. Come home and I'm sure Aunt Cis will give you a meal, I expect you've had a long day. Are you hungry?' As if hunger mattered! As if anything mattered. I had even quite forgotten the swan. Rick was safely back, and that was the whole of it.

We chatted as we walked back to the shop, but I'm not sure what about. My mind was full of worry about the swan, but I kept up with Rick's description of London and the ancient house he had to find. 'Miles from the nearest tube station, and I got there in the middle of lunchtime. Mr van Bruern was having a meal, which was embarrassing. But he was a nice old guy — invited me to share his lasagne, and yes, it was good. And we talked — my goodness, he knows his subject. I learned so much. His knowledge of silver is amazing . . . '

And then, suddenly, I could stand it no longer. I stopped in the middle of the pavement, pulled Rick round to look at me and said in too shrill a voice, 'And the swan — have you got the swan? And is it valuable? For heaven's sake, tell me, can't you?' Then, the moment the words left me, I knew I was behaving like a child; I felt my cheeks colour, turned away from Rick's amazed eyes, and began walking again. 'Sorry,' I said, very quietly, 'but you've been on my mind all day. Yes, I know I'm being stupid. Sorry, Rick.' And went along as fast as I could, finally reaching the shop and opening the back entrance, trying not to look at him as he followed me in.

Thank goodness for Aunt Cis and her constant calmness. 'Welcome back, Rick,' she said, and at once I felt the quiet words and serenity cool me down. I went into the kitchen, leaving them talking there in the front of the shop, and busied myself putting on potatoes and laying the table for four instead of three. Where Nigel had got to I had no idea, and quite honestly I didn't much care. He could get his supper somewhere else this evening, if it meant a few hours without his incessant chatter and broaching of new, ridiculous, ideas.

I didn't realize it, but Rick was taking Aunt Cis out to the stable yard and was talking to her about the empty shed which he seemed to think might make a first-rate workshop if she would take him on as a tenant. I heard the last few words of their conversation as I dished up the supper and then came back into the kitchen.

'Have to do something about the windows, of course,' Rick said, looking at Aunt Cis with what I recognized as determination on his face. 'But I'll see to that. And I could have a separate entrance so that you wouldn't be bothered. I could come and go without you even knowing. What do you think, Mrs Bartlett?'

Aunt Cis dished out the lamb stew and I piled vegetables on our plates, my ears flapping as I slowly understood what was in the air. Rick with his own workshop here? Right next door? I smiled a secret smile, and then banished it as I thought the scheme through. Yes, Rick would be all right, working away next door, but what if he brought his girl-friend with him? I had definite thoughts about Charlotte Sothern getting her grip into him — when I looked through the notebook for a second time I had found a tiny etching of Charlie right on the first page, and if that didn't mean some sort of connection, what did? And having Charlie living here, under my nose? No, thank you.

'Will you have some mashed swede, Rick?' I asked very formally. I didn't smile when he looked at me and grinned as he said, 'Yes, please. And perhaps I could persuade you to smile again, Mel? I know it's the swan that you want to know about, so I'll tell you what happened today. Well . . . ' And he was off, back in London, making his way to a distant tube station and then walking a good half mile to Mr van Bruern's ancient house out in the sticks.

While all this went on I toyed with my lamb and mashed swede and thought I never wanted to eat again. I wanted to hear about the swan . . .

'What a guy,' said Rick enthusiastically, passing his plate for a second helping. 'He knows so much about old silver — I'd give a lot to share even a bit of his knowledge.' He gave me another keen stare. 'But I'm afraid you must be patient for a bit longer, Mel. You see, the swan could — or might — be one of several ancient artefacts that have gone missing over the years. And even one would bring in a good sum, if found. So he's going to do more research. But, you see, there's also the possibility that it might be a fake.'

I discovered then that I had been holding my breath, which now came out in a noisy swoosh, making both Rick and Aunt Cis look at me with surprise. But no words followed. Instead I just stared at my plate and tried to eat what was left, and then found I couldn't. I put my knife and fork together and sat stiffly back in my chair. 'I see,' was all I could manage to say.

Aunt Cis recovered quickly. 'Well, at least that's honest, Rick,' she said, and took his empty plate, replacing it with a slice of apple pie and a large dollop of clotted cream. 'Get this inside you,' she said, smiling, 'and then perhaps you can think about Mel and her frustration. For I know she has one thing she's longing to ask you, but can't bring herself to do so.' She looked at me and nodded encouragingly. 'Say what you want to say, Mel, and stop being such a drama queen.'

Drama queen! I nearly bit my tongue for it was so completely what I wasn't feeling. But then Rick's amused eyes caught mine and I realized how foolishly I was behaving.

I eased my tense shoulders, and took a big breath. Then I faced him, and said, quietly, and with enormous control which pleased me very much, 'And of course you've brought back the swan, haven't you, Rick?'

I thought he looked at me rather strangely and at once my inner mind whispered, 'He hasn't got it — where is it? I don't believe he's a thief, but where is it?' And I was stiffening in my chair, getting ready to fly at him when the door behind us opened and in burst Nigel.

'Supper already?' he said. 'A bit early, isn't it? I was down there, talking to an old woman who knows all the town legends, and they were fascinating, but I suppose I stayed too long. I didn't really think I'd be late. Hope you've left me some. Sorry, Aunt Cis — I'll get another chair, shall I?' And as he turned to find another seat, he suddenly saw Rick sitting opposite. He frowned and stared at him.

'So you're back after all — well, I didn't expect to see you, but still . . . ' He found a chair and pulled it beside Rick, sitting down and looking around for a clean plate and clearly waiting to be served with his late meal.

I got up, and found immense pleasure in looking at the empty casserole and saying, 'Sorry, Nigel, nothing left. Bread and cheese do you?'

But Aunt Cis frowned at me, and pushed the apple pie — half of it left — towards him, saying, 'Tuck into this,

Nigel. Here's some cream, and Mel will find you a plate. Yes, and have some cheese with it — that'll fill you up.' She gave me a long disapproving stare which sent me back to the kitchen to find a pudding plate and the cheese-board and the biscuit tin. Wretched Nigel, I thought as I did all this. And coming in just when we were going to talk about the swan. I plonked the cheeseboard in front of him, and watched him helping himself to a huge chunk of apple pie, and then, with his mouth full, he asked the very question I was bravely trying to bring myself to ask.

'Well, quite a surprise to see you,' he mumbled, 'but brought the swan back safely, did you, then, Rick?'

9

I felt pinned to the floor, simply waiting for what would happen next. And, of course, it was bad feeling that at once struck up between the two men. Rick scraped back his chair, glowered down at Nigel, still eating his apple pie, with a blob of cream on his mouth, and growled, 'And what does that mean exactly? I need a straight answer . . . '

I willed Nigel to apologize, to somehow forge a better feeling between them, but no, he frowned, and his eyes narrowed into dark slits. 'You know what it means. That you walked off with the silver swan, and you haven't answered my question — where is it now?' He scooped up the last bit of pie, pushed back his chair and stood staring at Rick, the two of them just a foot apart.

I watched Rick controlling his anger,

backing off a step or two, and then looking apologetically at Aunt Cis, standing there with the coffee pot in her hand. 'Sorry, Mrs Bartlett. I don't want to make trouble, but this — lout — '

His scowl at Nigel was surely enough to make a lesser man tremble, but Nigel simply scowled back, his hand tense on the back of his chair, and I thought, well, at least he's not the coward I imagined him to be, but I don't want them to fight . . .

Words jumped into my mouth and I put a hand on Rick's arm, felt the muscle tense and strong beneath his sleeve. 'For goodness sake,' I said, and somehow forced a little laugh, 'this is all very uncalled for. I mean, Nigel was simply asking a question, and surely there's no need to take exception to it, Rick. After all, you HAVE got the swan, haven't you?'

He looked at me with those pale, suddenly icy eyes, and said, very quietly in his deep voice, 'And you have to ask me that, Mel? So you didn't trust me, taking it off like I did?'

My heart was beating too fast, I felt ashamed, and yet, no, I couldn't answer it truly. How could I possibly say what I felt — no, I didn't really trust you . . . thank goodness, then for Aunt Cis, firmly pushing her way to the table, putting down the coffee pot land saying in her calm voice, 'I think it's time to cool down and discuss this sensibly. Mel, get the mugs and sugar, please, then pour the coffee, and Nigel, you can put the rest of that apple pie in the fridge. Rick, perhaps a breath of fresh air while you and I take another look at the stable outside?' And slowly everything returned to normal.

When they returned to the kitchen I was washing up and good old Nigel was doing his best with the tea towel. I smiled at Rick, who looked at me warily, then smiled carefully, and said, 'I've told Mrs Bartlett that the swan is still in London with Mr van Bruern; he intends to bring it down as soon as he's finished his research. He wants to see some of my work.'

I threw away the dirty water, swirled out the sink and then turned and looked very straight at him. 'Rick,' I said, 'I'm sorry about everything that's happened. It wasn't necessary, I know it now. Please forgive me?'

Nigel disappeared upstairs and Aunt Cis went back to her counter in the shop. Rick and I were alone. His cold eyes thawed and he nodded at me. 'It's all right, Mel. We all have our doubts, don't we? And the swan is important, I know that. So can you wait a few days longer? It'll be back with you as soon as van Bruern comes down here.'

I walked slowly to the back door and opened it. 'Tell me what Aunt Cis said about the shed — oh, and I must give you back your notebook. I'll go and fetch it . . . '

But he was there at my side, hand on my arm, stopping me. 'Keep it,' he said simply. 'Until the swan comes back. Yes, really, I'd rather you did that.' He stopped for a moment, his gaze looking

straight into my eyes. 'Trust's important, isn't it, Mel? For you?'

Emotion swept through me, my
cheeks coloured and I turned away to
stop him seeing just how I felt. Of
course I trusted him. Didn't I? But then
Tony was in my mind, and his quick
partnership with another girl, forgetting
me, leaving me alone and lacking in
trust. I heaved a big sigh, looked down
at the floor and whispered, 'I'm sorry,
Rick. I'm a bit of a mess. I didn't mean
to suspect you.'

Silence for a few seconds, his hand
still on my arm. And then his low voice,
close to me, saying very quietly, 'I
understand. And we'll let it go, shall
we? For the moment.'

We looked at each other, and all I
could do was nod and hope my eyes
didn't show the tears pricking behind
them. Then his wonderful smile eased
his face, and he said, in a lighter, more
casual voice, 'And don't forget the party
on Friday evening. I've finished the
bracelet, just needs the last touches

now. I'll take it with me and give it to Charlie.' Another pause, and then, almost a whisper, 'You'll come with me, won't you, Mel?'

The tears disappeared, my body felt easier and lighter, and I smiled at him with all my heart when I replied, 'Of course I will, Rick. I'll see you at the Sotherns' about seven-thirty, shall I?'

He turned to the open door, and took a step outside. 'No, I'll come and collect you. And Mel, think about this shed out here, will you? It would make a great workshop if I did some alterations and I don't think Mrs Bartlett is against the idea . . . '

Charlie, I thought. Charlie and Rick together . . . but I smiled brightly, and said, 'Yes, I'll think about it, Rick.' And then watched him give me a last smile, before pulling his bag onto his shoulder and striding away up the street. I went upstairs and sat on my bed, and thought about what had happened in the last half hour. And wished I hadn't said all those hurtful things.

The next morning I went to see Sue in her shop. She was busy with a couple of customers, and told me quietly to put the kettle on and sit down and wait for her to be free. I did so, watching how good she was with people, how she charmed them into trying on the lovely vintage clothes they chose from her rails and shelves, and felt I was learning a good lesson which I would practise with my own small business.

At last she was free, and she made coffee which we sat and sipped while we chatted. Then she smiled at me, and said quietly, 'Any reason for calling, Mel? Everything going well? I imagine the new boutique is nearly ready — just over a week to opening day, isn't it? And how's Mrs Bartlett and her shop?'

I thought for a moment, then put down my cup, and said slowly, 'Aunt Cis is amazing. So strong, so calm. So different from me — I want to argue with Nigel all the time, and then Rick came back from London yesterday, and, and . . . ' I stopped, shook my head and looked away from her direct gaze.

'Problems?' she asked.

I thought about it for a long moment. Then — 'I as good as told him I didn't trust him. It was awful. And I felt terrible. Because I do believe he'll bring the swan back, but it's all because of Tony, who left me and then found another girl in about three weeks and forgot me.' I cleared my husky throat and met her compassionate eyes. 'Sue, I can't get over it. Can't stop thinking I'll never trust anyone again.'

She said nothing for a long moment, then she bent and touched my hands. 'Of course you can, Mel. In fact, you're the only person who can do it — just you.'

I stared at her. 'But I need help — I can't do it alone . . . '

'It's very simple. You just need to think differently. Even to tell yourself that you're learning new things.' Her smile was easy but I shook my head, not understanding.

111

'You're telling me to learn? And here I am, nearly twenty-nine — how can I possibly learn new tricks?'

Sue's smile was very amused. 'Simply tell yourself to. Like, I can decorate this old hat to make it pretty — or even, I can keep Rick in my mind as being someone completely reliable.'

'But that won't work — how can it?'

'Didn't you make the old hat quite beautiful?'

I felt confused. 'Yes, but that was different — a hat isn't part of me, is it?'

'It could be. Try it and see, Mel. Put Rick in your mind and see him with a halo around his long dark hair — that should do it.' Now she was actually laughing.

I sat there in silence, the coffee cooling in my cup and slowly her words began to make sense. It was me who had to make the difference, not Rick himself. And, yes, I would try . . . Very slowly, I said, 'I'll try, Sue. If you really think — '

A new customer came in then and she stood up, smiling a welcome, but finding just a second to whisper towards me, 'So go and do it. Go on.'

Then they were busy in the rails, looking for something rather special, and she gave me a last smile as I slipped out of the shop, on my way home and thinking very hard about her advice.

And almost at once it was Friday again and market morning, and we were busily driving up to the square with all Aunt Cis's bits and pieces, and I was thinking about what I would wear that evening at the Sotherns' party. I held Rick in my mind, like Sue had said, and thought about how he would be feeling, taking his bracelet to Charlotte and suddenly it came to me that he needed to trust her when he gave it to her. He would want to know that she really liked it; that she would wear it and not just keep it in a jewellery box upstairs, forgetting the man who made it for her; and how he worked so hard on selecting gemstones that would go with her eyes, and that the silver chain must have her initials on it. In fact, he had made it for Charlotte with a deep trust that she would love it, and respect all his hard work.

Trust. Yes, Sue had got it right. And I needed to do the same — to tell myself that the swan would return and that Rick had done a lot of personal work to help us value it. I left the antique stall with Aunt Cis's permission, and went down to the river to the workshop where I knew Rick would be putting last touches to the bracelet.

* * *

I had a chat with Gary, and then Rick came up to me, smiling, looking into my eyes, as he said, 'This is a nice surprise. And what are you doing here? Thought you'd be up with your aunt and the antiques?'

I took a deep breath, looked at him for a moment that seemed to stretch on as I realized the kindness and the generosity that filled his face. And I felt a new sensation spread gently through me, promising to fill me with warmth and pleasure, as I said, quietly, and not making a fuss, 'Just wanted to make sure you are all right. That the bracelet is finished and that you really do want me to go with you this evening.'

'But I asked you — and you said yes ... ' He looked surprised for a moment and moved me out of Gary's workshop into the sunshine outside. His pale eyes were soft. 'So what's all this about, Mel?' We walked to the bench, as before, and sat down, and he turned and looked at me with concern. 'What've I done?' he asked, frowning.

And I felt the start of something new growing inside me. I wasn't sure what it was, but I said, very quietly, and with a smile that slowly spread, 'You've done just what I wanted you to do, Rick, and everything's just fine. I'd like to think we can forget last night?'

He nodded, and I watched his expression change until his smile was as warm as mine, as he said, deep, and very quiet, like a magical bar of intimate music, 'That just about suits me, Mel. Start again from here, perhaps?'

I nodded, and I felt a great weight start to release itself from my body. And it was a wonderful feeling.

10

Such excitement, dressing for the Sotherns' party. I felt like a young girl, going on her first spree, but knew I must behave according to my age. Twenty-nine, and sensible, or so I hoped. Nigel was grumbling that he hadn't been invited, so we had to try and calm him down. Aunt Cis suggested he might like a short trip on a boat down the river to a much-respected inn further down.

'You'll have a good dinner, and there will be lots of interesting people there,' she said, looking sideways at me and daring me to laugh. I went up to my room feeling very content with life today, and tried to choose what to wear.

I had mixed thoughts. Several people might by now know that Silver Swan Crafts was opening next week and would even look at me to see how I dressed. Should I be resplendent in my best vintage gown? Or perhaps something a little more subtle which might make people talk more? And did I want them to talk? Well, of course . . . business was about to start and so I must find the same smiling, but efficient image I had had in London with Lissa. And yet, this time the business would be mine alone. Yes, mine . . .

I stood in front of the mirror and looked at what I had selected to wear. A calf-length plain but beautiful jade-green-coloured 1960s dress that had once been on a famous catwalk. I paired it with flesh-coloured tights, plain court shoes that didn't show any age, and, for the sake of vintage itself, a rather lovely chunky long string of glass beads in a pale turquoise colour, which moved about and caught the light as I moved. After a few minutes of careful deliberation, I thought I looked all right. And then I remembered that Rick was collecting me; we were going to walk up the hill and so to the Sotherns' house. In these shoes? I replaced them with my flatties and decided to carry the courts in a small, elegant little bag.

I took one last look at my reflection as I heard the kitchen clock strike half seven, and then went downstairs, ready to greet Rick. As I paused by the kitchen door, I wondered what he might be wearing. The old jacket? A slightly thread-bare shirt? Oh dear — and I was smiling to myself as he appeared in the yard, because by now I was fond of his arty appearance. I didn't want him to change.

So who was this attractive, well-groomed chap who stood before me? I know my mouth fell open and I quickly said, 'You've cut your hair.'

One dark eyebrow went up. 'So? I thought it was necessary. Hope you approve?'

'I'm — er — not sure . . . '

'Or the freshly cleaned jacket? And the new shirt? Come on, Mel, give a bit of praise where it's due.'

I was shocked. This was a new Rick,

just as handsome, perhaps even more so now that small ears and back of neck were visible. But where was my untidy silversmith with the shabby clothes, swirling hair that glinted in the sun and the old shirts that I was becoming quite fond of? I swallowed my dismay, and said, 'Well, at least you look clean,' and then thought how dreadful that sounded. I bit my lip and stared at him, and, thank goodness, his wonderful smile broke through, none the worse for having a makeover.

'For a moment I thought you wouldn't come with me. But, you see, an occasion needs cleanliness sometimes. And Charlie's birthday definitely does. Well, I can't dance with her with dust all over me, can I? Come on, Mel, give me a word of praise for doing the right thing . . . '

So I nodded, mumbled something about handsome is as handsome does, as I picked up my bag, went out of the door in front of him and walked out into the street. But I was thinking — so the Sotherns demanded a different Rick. It struck me with a disappointment that I didn't enjoy. Wasn't he good enough for them in his old clothes? He had been good enough for me; for old Mr van Bruern in London, and even for Aunt Cis. (If not quite right for Nigel.) But not the Sotherns . . .

We walked up the hill and then down the small valley leading to the big house and we talked about the weather, about the new boutique opening on Friday, and finally, about Charlie's bracelet. Rick took it out of his pocket, unwrapped, just a beautiful silver chain jewel, with the fading sun glinting on lapis lazuli and citrines, and I admired it. I wished it was going to be mine — but then told myself Charlie was someone who meant a lot to Rick, and so he had made this exquisite bracelet for her. I mustn't be envious.

And by the time we reached the house, with its terrace lit with Chinese lanterns, and people standing about, talking and laughing, my gloom was almost gone. I was at a party. I intended to enjoy myself. I smiled at Mrs Sothern and Charlie when I was introduced and wished her a happy birthday. And I watched as Rick took the bracelet out of his pocket and handed it over. I noticed particularly his smile, saw his eyes look warm and generous, and told myself painfully that he had a soft spot for Charlie. But what did it matter to me?

I listened to Mrs Sothern's exclamation of admiration as she saw Charlie place it on her arm, and I saw Charlie's expression as she held out her arm to Rick, who carefully locked the small latch, finally watching her smile grow into a huge beam of pleasure.

'It's gorgeous! Thank you, Rick, what a beauty it is. Mother, aren't you pleased?'

And Mrs Sothern, casting an eye on Rick, then returning Charlie's smile, as she said carefully, 'A beautiful present, darling. How lucky you are. And Rick, I do congratulate you on that fine work.

We must have a word about it later on.'

So, I thought, things were pretty plain. Rick had an eye for Charlie who definitely had feelings for him. Well, that was all right by me. I had a new business and was feeling fairly happy down here in Stretton. Not so noisy as London. Not so crowded. And then there was the possibility of making a few thousand through Aunt Cis's silver swan and so setting my business plan in action.

I slowly wandered away down the terrace, leaving Mrs Sothern, Charlie and Rick talking under the Chinese lanterns. I would find other, interesting people, perhaps a thoughtful man or two, to chat to. Even to dance with — there would be music, and I saw the small group in the big room behind the terrace getting their instruments ready. Lovely. I would dance — but must put on my smart court shoes. I was in a small anteroom, changing them, when suddenly Rick appeared in the doorway. He looked at me in a strange way. 'You disappeared,' he said. 'Why did you go?'

I put my flat shoes in my bag and stowed it on an empty shelf. 'I had to change my shoes so that I can dance. And anyway, you were busy with Charlie and her mother. They liked the bracelet, didn't they?'

He stopped me going out of the door, one arm stretched over the entrance to the room. 'Mel — ' Something in his voice I hadn't heard before.

'Yes, Rick?'

'What's wrong?'

I put a smooth smile on my face and looked into his pale eyes, suddenly slightly narrowed and very direct. 'Nothing's wrong! What should be? I told you, just had to change my shoes.'

He took my arm, drew me towards him and made sure I stayed there. 'Tell me.'

For the first time I felt uncertain about my feelings. I had thought I could live without a man, busying myself with family, friends and business. But now, to be so near him, to hear him breathe, feel the strength of his hand on my arm, was dangerous. Men were dangerous. I had thought I could do without one. I wrenched my hand away, gave him a bit of a push, and escaped from the little room.

'Sorry,' I said as I almost ran, 'but someone asked me to dance, and I must go and find him . . . ' I crossed my fingers, threw a bright smile behind me and went into the gathering crowd of dancers, standing around the terrace and the lawn outside, listening to the music and already moving in time with the captivating rhythm. Surely, I thought, someone will dance with me? So then he can go back to Charlie.

He let me go. I caught a glimpse of him slowly walking back towards Charlie, waiting with an expectant smile on her pretty face. She looked lovely, I thought, as I began dancing, and hoping for a partner to find me. Her gown was expensive and the pastel satin suited the pallor of her face and the rich brown of her long, curling hair. Rick could do much worse than pair up with Charlie Sothern, I thought. And even as I thought so, a man held out a hand to me, grinned, and said, 'All on your own? Too bad — like to join me?' And then I was being held, twisted around, finding the old pleasure of dancing, and hoping that Rick saw me having such a good time with another man.

The evening went on, and my emotions slowly grew back under control. I danced with Mike for what seemed a long time; enjoying the music and the dance, and being part of a jolly crowd again, until my feet started aching, and I was thirsty and out of breath. Twenty-nine, I thought, with comic dismay. I need a rest.

Luckily Mike thought so too. He steered me out of the dancing mob, and sat me down on a handy chair at the end of the terrace. 'Like a drink? I'll get us one. Stay there.' And he disappeared back into the house where a bar was functioning.

I began thinking about going home.

Shadows filled the garden, couples were wandering through the trees, the music had stopped briefly, a half moon shone down and I knew I had had enough. It might be difficult to shelve nice Mike, after dancing with him all the evening — better if I just disappeared. He'd soon find someone else to have my drink. So I got up and walked into the half light of the garden.

The coolness, the sudden quietness, was wonderful, and I found a small seat at the end of a long summer border, full of tall, beautiful flowers and fragrant shrubs, and sat there, calming down. I waited anxiously, watching people as they strolled between the woodlands and the colourful flowerbed, but Mike didn't appear, and I was glad. He would have found someone else quite easily — he was a nice man, and I was grateful to him for dancing with me. But we didn't need to meet again.

After all, I had told myself earlier that I had no need of a particular man. The business and Aunt Cis would be enough — and then, Nigel . . . I was smiling a bit as I thought of him, and hoped he had enjoyed the river trip. But would he ever find that elusive new job?

I had rested enough, and now I knew I must return to the house, find my walking shoes and start on the journey home. Indeed, I was just walking through the small stand of silver birch trees which shone in the moonlight, when someone said my name.

'Mel.'

I spun round and saw Rick standing there in the small moonlit space in front of the trees. At once my calmness died and I was full of thoughts — what to say? What to do? Where to go? But no words came and I just stood there, like a statue turned to stone.

He came closer, looked deeply into my eyes, and said, very quietly, very low, 'You left me. You found someone else. I saw you dancing. Why did you do that?'

'Because — ' I stepped backwards from him, wanting to run, but unable to go because I needed my shoes from the anteroom. How silly was that? I felt like a gauche schoolgirl and was embarrassed by my foolishness. I cleared my throat. 'Because you needed to dance with Charlie, of course. You didn't want to have to bother with me. And anyway I found someone called Mike — a nice guy — we danced together very well, but then I got tired, and, and thirsty, and, you see, now I have to go and change my shoes before I go home.' I stopped, tried not to look into his eyes, and added unsteadily, 'So I'll just go and find them . . . '

'Mel, stop.'

I could do nothing else, slowly turning away from him, needing to go but lacking the strength to do so when that deep voice said stop. Then he was beside me, close, arms reaching out to hold me. I shouldn't be doing this but the temptation to give in was far too great to escape. I closed my eyes.

11

We stood, as one person, very near to each other with just his arms round my waist. No kisses. No close embrace, just this feeling of strength and reassurance which to me, in that amazing moment, was so very important. Here was someone who understood me, yet allowed me the freedom I felt I must have. And so, slowly, all my confidence returned. Yes, I was Mel, with a new business ready to take off, with the hope of the silver swan perhaps financing my future, and with Aunt Cis and her shop all around me. I felt there was nothing else I needed.

Until I opened my eyes and found Rick looking at me with enormous warmth. He let a few moments slide past, and then, quietly, with a smile of amusement, said, 'Feeling better? Then I'll find your shoes and we'll be off home. Where are they?'

And then it all flooded back. Rick and Charlie. His involvement with the Sothern family. His burgeoning career. And his kindly interest in our silver swan. His research, the time he was spending finding out about my swan. The time he should be working away at his silver-making. I had no right to take up his time like this. So I stepped away, found a smile from somewhere, and said, rather huskily, 'In the anteroom. In my little bag. How kind of you, Rick.' And watched him nod, look at me with concern in his eyes that were shining so clearly in the moonlight, before he turned, and walked back through the trees towards the terrace and the house. I knew what I must do; I turned and ran down the drive to the road, caught a lucky taxi waiting in the main street and was driven back to the antique shop, where I saw Aunt Cis's bedroom light still on, waiting for me to return.

I tiptoed up the stairs, but she heard

me and called out, 'All right, Mel?'

So I went to her door, opened it a slip, stuck my head into her room, summoned up a big smile, and said, 'Yes, Aunt Cis. Had a lovely time. Tell you about it in the morning.'

She nodded, switched off her bedside light, and I saw her settle down among the pillows, looking relaxed. Then I went to my own room and tried to tell myself I had done the best thing regarding Rick. He wasn't for me, so just get on with life. Like Sue said, 'Keep living.'

But in the morning, when I opened the back door to fetch in the milk, there was my bag, and my shoes, on the step. And inside the bag, a small note. 'Be seeing you soon. R.'

I looked at the writing, saw approvingly how elegant his hand was; knew that I was still wishing the evening had gone differently, when Nigel came rushing downstairs, and then Rick and his charms took a different turn.

'How is she this morning?' asked Nigel, staring at me with a frown on his face.

I filled the kettle and put it on the hob. 'How is who?'

'Aunt Cis, of course. She fell last night, getting off that boat — said, no it wasn't bad, just a slight sprain, but she was limping quite badly when we got home. I said I would take her to the hospital but of course, she wouldn't have that. And I'm afraid she might be feeling a bit more pain today.'

At once I was halfway up the stairs, and yes, she was trying to get out of bed, but her face told me just how bad the sprain was. 'So silly of me,' she complained, 'the boat sort of juddered, and I was off balance. Oh, don't worry, dear, it will soon be better. Perhaps you might bring me up your uncle's walking stick, down in the hallway? I can get about with that . . . '

Now I had something to switch off my mind from Rick Martin, and thank goodness for it. I said very firmly, 'I'll drive you to the hospital and they can see what's to be done. Don't argue, Aunt Cis.' And a useful thought slipped into my mind. 'Nigel can mind the shop while we're gone.'

It turned out to be a bad sprain which needed resting and very gentle exercise. Certainly no running a shop for a while. Between us, Nigel and I told her that we should look after everything and she must simply sit and rest. Soon she would be back to normal again. But of course, Aunt Cis was never one to do nothing. So we left her in the kitchen, sitting at the table, weighing out sugar and butter for another load of flapjacks. 'I can manage, stop worrying,' she told us, and literally swept us out of the room. I looked at Nigel as we returned to the shop, and he looked at me, and then I saw how his eyes were gleaming.

'I'll take over the antiques,' he said airily, 'and you can get on with your old clothes. I mean the vintage stuff.' He almost pushed me into my little boutique, saying, 'I'll soon pick up how to deal with everything, I've got a good business head, so just leave me to it, Mel.'

He didn't do badly. One or two requests floored him and we had to go and ask Aunt Cis, now sitting listening to her radio while the flapjacks cooked, and she enlightened him. But when he'd gone back to the shop, and I saw him searching through cupboards and shelves as if looking for something, she nodded at me, and said very firmly, 'I shall be back in a day or two. I don't want him messing up my books, although I know he's being very kind and helpful. Yes, a day or two will be more than enough, thank you.'

★　★　★

How fast the days went by after that. Nigel and I somehow managed to deal with Aunt Cis's antiques, and I worked at the final details of my new boutique. I had no time to think about anything except the passing minute, and then, suddenly and unexpectedly, it was Thursday afternoon and tomorrow would bring the opening date of Silver Swan Crafts.

By now Aunt Cis was hobbling around the house, her will power insisting that her ankle was nearly better. 'Don't look so worried,' she said at breakfast time on Friday, 'I shan't be going to the market. There's too much to do here, because of course, Mel, you'll have troops of customers coming in and needing attention. And I shall make coffee and biscuits . . . ' Her smile was reassuring, and so I told Nigel that the market was off.

I wondered why he looked suddenly downcast, and said quickly that he had something important to do, so couldn't be around to help me this morning. If only I had thought about it . . . but all I could put my mind to was the Opening with a big O. Allegra had already arrived as we finished breakfast and was fussing around in my new little room, lighting candles, rearranging clothes which I had already arranged, putting a disk of dreamy music on the CD player, and generally making herself a handy helper. And then, gratefully, I realized she had done her work very well, and on the dot of ten o'clock I heard voices outside the shop door, which I hurried to open.

I was delighted to see that dear Aunt Cis had used her watercolours again, this time to paint a beautiful silver swan swimming on a jade-green lake, with trees hanging in the background, and sun gleaming on the water. She had fixed it on the inside of the shop window and in large capitals she had printed 'Silver Swan Crafts'. Just what we needed, I thought, and hurried to tell her so and to thank her. And, thanks to Allegra's publicity, and that evocative sign in the window, a small crowd had gathered, chatting and laughing among themselves, and so I invited them in. 'Please try and make yourselves comfortable — not an awful lot of room — but my clothes are all around so you can have a good look.'

Allegra sat on a stool by my side, behind the small, decorated table, and whispered, 'I think you'll do quite well.

Look who's here — Mrs Sothern and her daughter. Now, that's a real catch.' Charlie and her mother were looking through the rails and I caught Charlie's glance. She saw me looking, nodded, and then came up to the table. 'Interesting old things, Mel, and Mother's looking at everything.' And then, she turned away, saying over her shoulder, 'Enjoy yourself last night, did you? I saw you dancing with Mike Braithwaite — such a nice guy. Going to keep up with him, are you?'

A shadow darkened my thoughts. Was my name about to be joined to his? What might Rick think about that? I said, very firmly, 'Yes, it was a really good party. But no, I shan't be seeing Mike again. Now, have you looked at the blouses over there, in front of those shelves? Some gorgeous Edwardian high-necked ones — would suit you, very well.'

We looked at each other and she gave me a supercilious faint smile. 'I'm not into Edwardian, it's today I'm interested in, and elegant bridal gowns. I'm only here because Mother wanted to come,' she added sharply, and turned away, but not before I had seen her look towards her mother, and nod her head towards the door. So that would be that. Something in her that didn't want to know me, and quite honestly I felt the same about her. Except that we had shared thoughts of one man in our lives — Rick Martin.

By lunch time I was exhausted. Allegra's help had been wonderful, the customers had been very keen on my clothes, and the small till was growing increasingly full. Aunt Cis had made soup for our lunch and was telling me to put a closed notice on the door.

'Come in here and relax, Mel. You've been on the go for nearly three hours — and I wonder where Nigel has got to? I'll keep the soup hot. It's leek and potato — his favourite, I know.'

We had a quiet lunch, with Aunt Cis worrying about Nigel, and making sure she kept the soup ready for his return. But it was Sue Bennett who appeared at the shop door when we opened again in the afternoon. She came in and spent a little time in the boutique with me, glancing through the rails, and complimenting me on the atmosphere and elegance of the little room.

Then she said, quietly, but with a look that told me it wasn't exactly good news, 'Did you know your cousin Nigel was thinking of starting his own business in the market? He was there this morning, talking to Allegra Smith, and she told me he was keen to start selling jewellery and silver. I didn't know he was experienced — is he?'

I caught my breath. So that's what he was up to; taking advantage of running Aunt Cis's shop for a couple of days, and now thinking he could start on his own. But — sell silver? What on earth did he know about that? And then one after the other, thoughts rushed in. Looking for Uncle Denys's old books. And the silver swan; was he taking it on himself to do some research? And Rick's notebook, which I hadn't returned to him. It must still be somewhere here — or was it? Had Nigel taken it to learn from Rick's designs, and so give him something to talk about when he started up his own stall? I jumped up and went to find Aunt Cis. 'Where is Rick Martin's notebook?' I asked, and she looked up from behind her counter.

'Didn't you return it to him last night? I found it was missing when I went to look and imagined you had already taken it.' She frowned, and I knew she was guessing, as I had done, that Nigel was behind this latest little bit of skulduggery. She added, frowning, that he had been rummaging around among Uncle Denys's silver assay mark books, but I managed a smile. Her ankle was still painful, although she was getting about with the walking stick, and I didn't want to worry her any more.

'I expect it's around somewhere,' I said airily. 'I'll have a good look and then return it to Rick when I've got a moment. Perhaps this evening . . . '

I found Sue sorting through some

gemstone rings, and admiring a couple of Lissa's 1950s dance dresses. 'You should do well with all these lovely things, Mel,' she said. 'I heard one or two people talking about being here this morning, and they were really full of admiration. And it's such a lovely name — Silver Swan Crafts. Does that mean you will set up other craft stalls here, as well as yours and Mrs Bartlett's?' I thought about Rick wanting the old stable, and didn't answer for a moment. But I knew Charlie would hate to be here, in an old, dusty sort of building, and so I cleared my mind of the idea, and returned Sue's smile.

'Who knows?' I said. 'Like you said, Sue, live for the day and just wait and see what happens.'

She nodded, and said she must go. 'See you again soon, Mel. And don't forget the craft competition next week.'

I had done, but now it came rushing into my head. Perhaps Mr van Bruern would have been in touch with Rick before then; perhaps I should see Rick there. Perhaps we should have news of the swan. Perhaps it would be very good news . . . ?

But what happened next, as I bade goodbye to Sue, was that Nigel came rushing into the shop, his face shining with excitement.

'I'm going into selling,' he said very loudly, and with a huge grin on his face. 'I've learned about selling antiques from Aunt Cis and all about silver from Uncle Denys, so now I'm going into it on my own. I must tell you all about it!'

12

We stared at him. And then Aunt Cis said sharply, 'What are you talking about, Nigel? Do you mean you're actually going to be a marketeer? Get a stall, and fill it with saleable objects? But what things? And where will you get them all from? I must say, it sounds very unlikely. Please explain yourself, my boy.'

She looked at me, and her frown said everything that I was thinking. Nigel was up to no good. Then a warning bell rang in my head, and I said, almost without more thought, 'Have you got Rick Martin's notebook? It's gone from where Aunt Cis put it, and I haven't taken it, so you must have done. Let me have it, please, Nigel.'

I watched his expression change from excitement to what looked like sullen guilt. But he said, at once, his voice very rough and cross, 'What a thing to say! Why accuse me? You're not being fair, either of you. I thought you'd both be so pleased that I'd found a decent job. But now — ' He stopped abruptly and glowered at me. I was just about to say something sensible about organising a stall and that goods to sell couldn't just start like that, it was bound to take time, when he went on, 'As it happens, I have got the wretched notebook. Aunt Cis told me to have a look at it, which I did, and suppose I must have put it back in my pocket instead of wherever her hiding place was.'

Aunt Cis and I exchanged shocked glances, and then he blustered, 'The way you're going on, you're making me out to be a thief, and I think that's really nasty of both of you. In fact, I shall be glad to leave here as soon as I can find a lodging somewhere.'

'And the sooner the better.' The words were out before I could stop them, and I had the grace to add, rather red-faced, 'Sorry, Nigel, but you aren't behaving very well, you know, and you're being a real worry to Aunt Cis. Which isn't good for her.' I met his angry stare without flinching, and held out my hand for the notebook.

'I'll take it to Rick this evening, and explain where it's been. I don't think he'll be too pleased, but perhaps you could drop in on him and apologize for the delay, Nigel?'

'I'll do no such thing. He should never have offered to let you see it in the first place.'

Silence for a few long moments while we avoided looking at each other, until finally Nigel flounced across the room and opened the shop door. 'Things to do. I'll be back in time for supper. That is, if I'm still welcome.' He smiled unpleasantly, and Aunt Cis tutted as he disappeared from view down the street, leaving us not quite sure what to do next.

I sighed heavily, put the notebook which he had almost thrown at me in my bag, and said sadly, 'He may be family, Aunt Cis, but he's quite irresponsible. Will he ever find the life he longs for?'

She echoed my sigh. 'Some people never do, Mel, but we must keep hoping. Do you think Rick Martin will make a fuss about him taking the notebook?'

I thought, and then said slowly, 'I'll try and make light of it. And I don't think Rick's likely to make a big deal out of it. After all, he lent it to me quite freely in the first place.'

Aunt Cis kept her keen eyes on my face. 'Yes, he did. Which must say that he trusts you, Mel, my dear. Think about that. When will you return it?'

I started to tidy up some scarves falling out of their box. Aunt Cis was too observant for me at this moment. 'As soon as I shut up shop this afternoon. I think he works quite late, so he'll still be down in his workshop.' And then I thought about Mr van Bruern, and all the dismay about Nigel and the notebook faded away for perhaps Rick would have news of the silver swan?

The evening was a glorious one and I took great delight in walking along the river bank towards the workshop. Seagulls swooped around a fishing boat which was unloading its catch of fish, and the light gently illumined the trees with softness. People were walking dogs, sitting on the benches dotted along the waterside, or slowly walking as if with no particular aim save to enjoy the evening.

Outside Rick's workshop I paused, for now was going to be difficult. I had to thank him properly for returning my shoes; and I hoped he had forgiven me for leaving the party so abruptly. What would he say when I went in and found him there, working? Would he be irritated at being disturbed, or would he be pleased to see me . . . ? I entered the workshop very quietly, and with my heart in my mouth.

He was there, a tall, burly figure leaning on Gary's table and gesticulating with one large hand. They both looked up as I entered, and I was greeted with smiles. 'Hi,' said Gary. 'Just been hearing about the party, a good do, apparently. And you were the belle of the ball, so he says . . . ' With a big grin he nodded at Rick, who looked embarrassed, but smiled all the same.

I waited for words to come, but couldn't think of anything, and then his deep voice said, 'You looked amazing in that simple dress, Mel — beat all the dressed up girls, including m'lady Charlie! I tried to find you, I wanted to dance, but you disappeared . . . '

I met his eyes and managed to smile. 'My feet called me away while you were chatting to the Sotherns,' I told him, and thank goodness, he nodded and looked as if he believed me. I felt my heartbeat return to normal and was able then to say, quite calmly, 'And it was so kind of you to return my shoes. I did appreciate it, Rick — thank you so much. And here's your notebook.' I handed it to him, watched while he flipped open the pages as if looking for something, and then told myself I must keep the business of Nigel studying it with a view to perhaps start copying his designs, until we were alone. And when would that be? I wondered.

'Got time for a wander down the river, Mel?'

The deep mellow voice melted all my worries and I looked at him gratefully. 'I'd love to.'

Gary switched on his music downloads as we left, and we grinned at each other as the rowdy music followed us quickly walking down the path beneath the trees. When, after a good walk, we found a sheltered spot beneath trees with a small, sandy beach, he said quietly, 'Have you thought any more about that workshop idea, Mel? I've really had enough of Gary's noise — I'm one of those people who need quiet to work in.' We sat down on the grass and he turned to look at me directly. 'I expect you've got a good reason why you say no, but — well — can we talk about it?'

I took a very deep breath, trying to work out how I could bring Charlie into this conversation. But he was looking at me so intently, waiting for my reply, that I could only stutter a few excuses. 'It would probably cost a lot, putting in bigger windows, and making good all the repairs that are needed.'

He didn't say anything for a moment, and then he smiled, almost as if he were amused, but also a bit anxious. 'Mel,' he said, quietly, his deep voice sending little drifts of pleasure around my mind, 'I think you're playing games with me. All this is rubbish — the cost, the repairs . . . why can't you tell me what's the real reason you don't want me to take on the stable as my workshop? Come on, you know we're friends, don't you? So why all the prevarication?'

I felt myself slowly allow all the tension that had been building to disappear as I realized the truth of his words. He was a man who would easily discuss all the matters relating to the stable conversion. There would be no hiding anything. And he expected me to be as truthful as he was. But — how could I say what I felt about Charlie?

Words chased about in my head, and finally I came out with a stuttered, 'It's something I find hard to talk about, Rick.'

He nodded as if he understood, then said quietly, 'So let me guess. If it's not the actual work that has to be done, it's perhaps something to do with me taking on the workshop. Maybe you don't like the idea of me being around your boutique every day — is that it?'

I caught my breath. 'No! Of course it's not that — Aunt Cis and I would both make you welcome, but — ' And then stopped abruptly as his frown warned me from uttering the name that trembled on my lips.

'But, Mel? Come on, what's the real problem?'

And then I knew I had to tell him. I looked down at the grass, so green and soft and welcoming, and feared he would get up and walk away once he knew what I was thinking. But he wanted the truth and I could do no less than tell him.

'I don't think Charlie would like you to be there.' The words were so quiet I feared he might not hear, but he did.

'Charlie Sothern? But I don't see what she'd have to do with my new workshop. What do you mean?'

He didn't understand, and I felt even more confused. I muttered something about, 'Well, she's in your notebook, so I thought perhaps — perhaps you were fond of her . . . ' I couldn't look at him, but pulled a handful of grass and played with it on my lap.

And then his hand was there, taking it away and throwing it into the river, where it slowly drifted out of sight. A moment's silence, and then he said, very quietly, 'But you're in the notebook as well, Mel. So does that mean I'm fond of you, too?'

That made me look up and meet his questioning eyes. 'I — don't know . . . '

And then he laughed and I felt myself grow taut and annoyed. Where was all this leading? And what did it tell me about him — and Charlie? And then, even more important, did I really want to know? But the seconds passed, with only the song of the chattering water and a blackbird singing further down the valley filling my mind. Until I knew I must find out, so slowly, I said, 'Rick, I don't understand why you're laughing. Have I said something funny?'

He smiled, a gentle expression that I felt was trying hard to make out what I was going on about. And then he said, 'Mel, you're a sort of creative artist, just like I am, so surely you understand that our minds work differently from other people's?'

I thought about my love of vintage clothes, and said carefully, 'Yes. I think about what I want to put in my boutique, how to arrange them, if I can make them look even more beautiful . . . '

'And that's just what I do with my notebook. I sketch things that catch my eye, trying to work out what I can do to make them look even better than they are at the moment.' He stopped, put out his hand and took mine, making me look at him again. 'I sketched Charlie because I wanted to discover the sort of girl she was; and therefore the type of jewellery she would want for her birthday present. That's fairly clear, isn't it?'

'Yes,' I said at once, my mind clearing. 'But what did you want to find out about me, Rick? Why put me in your creative notebook?'

I heard him sigh, frowned as he took my other hand and pressed them both together. His were warm, strong, and somehow reassuring, but I was still waiting for the truth. Then he said, 'I saw, not a interesting artifact that I wanted to enhance or copy, but a girl with a lovely face whose gentle voice told me that she knew what pain was. Perhaps I had it in mind to help her, in some way — in the future, if that was possible.'

I slid my hands out of his but was

mesmerized by the expression in his pale, unblinking eyes. I didn't know what to say, but almost at once he asked gently, 'Does that answer your question, Mel? And will it help you accept me as a possible tenant for your aunt's old stable?'

I nodded. I was in a state of unexpected pleasure. Yes, he understood me. Yes, he had answered my question truthfully. And I thought, with a little jump of hope, that perhaps, after all, Charlie and her quest for a bridal gown didn't really involve Rick Martin. All these things ran around in my mind, needing time and space to sort out. But not now. So I got to my feet, looked at my watch and said, 'Goodness, is that the time? I really must go home. And — er — when do you expect to hear from your Mr van Bruern, Rick? I do hope it will be soon. I'm so looking forward to hearing about the silver swan and its past.'

He got up and stood beside me, and we started walking back towards the town. 'Any time now, Mel,' he said, and from the expression in his voice, I knew that although he had told me the truth about the notebook, the silver swan was a controversial subject still to be considered in the future.

13

When the telephone behind Aunt Cis's counter rang, I hurried to answer it so that she wouldn't have to limp over there.

A man's voice spoke in a slightly foreign accent. 'Am I speaking to Mrs Bartlett? My name is Sebastien van Bruern, and I have an important matter to discuss with her.'

My heart began to pound. I asked, 'Can you hold on a minute while I find her? Just a moment, please . . . ' And I went to where Aunt Cis was sitting, examining some new pieces of porcelain she had just acquired. 'It's Mr van Bruern,' I said quickly, 'and he wants to talk to you. Can you reach the phone?'

She nodded, smiled and, with my helpful arm, propped herself up against a handy beam where she could take the receiver. I heard her voice, warm and welcoming, as she started talking, but I took myself off into the kitchen, thinking that this conversation was a private one, and if necessary, she would tell me about it afterwards.

Sebastien van Bruern! He sounded foreign, like a warmer Hercule Poirot, I thought, grinning to myself. And Rick had said his knowledge of silver was excellent — so what could he be saying to Aunt Cis? I supposed it was Rick who had given him our phone number. It was hard to make myself start making soup for lunch, while all the time wondering about what was being discussed in the shop.

At last Aunt Cis came in and sat down on one of the stools beside the table. I paused in my preparation of vegetables, and said, 'Well, what did he say? Has he told you anything about the swan?'

Aunt Cis smiled at me. 'Keep calm, dear child! We have to meet him for lunch tomorrow, and then he says he will tell us exactly what he has discovered. So

— no, we still don't know any more than we did previously.' She paused, then added, 'Don't give up hope, we may still be sitting on a fortune, you know!' But then she laughed, and I felt embarrassed for even imagining such a thing.

I said carefully, 'So where are you lunching with this important Mr van Bruern?'

'He's staying at the King William, in the town, and would like us — yes, you as well, of course — to be ready for him to collect us in his car at twelve noon tomorrow.' She stopped, and her smile faded. 'Perhaps Nigel will sit in for me as he did before. What do you think?'

'I'm not sure if you can trust him, Aunt Cis. He's very interested in all Uncle Denys's old papers and things, you know.'

She nodded pensively. 'I suppose it's this great idea of learning about silver that's got into him. Well, if he's really interested, perhaps it's a good thing. Could be a career of some sort.'

I gave a rather sarcastic little snort. 'He'll never stick to it, not Nigel. Something else will crop up and then that'll be the important thing.'

Aunt Cis got to her feet, shook her head at me, and said sharply, 'I can manage. You get on with the soup. I think we'll have a celebratory drink — there's some sauvignon blanc in the frig, I think . . . ' And she shuffled over the floor to the frig and found the half bottle while I got the glasses ready.

We drank a toast to Mr van Bruern, and then had our lunch, chatting as we did so, and planning a few vague, but amazing ideas, should the silver expert have good news for us. And then, just as we were clearing up, in came Nigel.

'Good news!' He beamed. 'I've been talking to the chap who sells the jewellery in the market, and keeps his stall going all the week. He can do with someone to help — and offers to teach me all he knows about making costume jewellery if I fill in for him when he has to leave the stall. So I'll be doing that from now on. No need to worry about me, I'll be out all day, and just come home to sleep.' His grin faded. 'Except for supper, of course — don't want to miss your lovely cooking, Aunt Cis!'

We looked at each other, and then she smiled at him, saying quietly, 'So another new idea, Nigel, and let's hope this is the one that will last. I have to say well done, my lad — and mind you keep at it. Now, how about a cup of coffee and a ham sandwich? I don't suppose you had any lunch, did you?'

And, of course, he sat down, looking pleased with himself and said yes, that'd be great. I went into the kitchen to clear up the lunch dishes, and try and keep myself calm about his extraordinary lack of clear vision. Where would cousin Nigel end up? I asked myself. And tried not to add that I hoped it would eventually be far away from Stretton.

The afternoon became busy, but I closed my little boutique at tea time, because I had to go into town and look for more vintage clothes, as my stock was running low. And, of course, I wondered if I might bump into Rick Martin.

I didn't see him, but Allegra Smith came rushing around a corner as I approached and we almost collided. 'Ah, Melody! Lovely to see you — have heard such good reports of your beautiful old clothes, so glad you're doing well. And what about that clever young cousin of yours, Nigel? Has he found the job he's looking for yet? And what about Rick Martin being discovered by the famous silver expert, someone called van Bruern? I hear he's come down to Stretton to offer him a job . . . '

I felt a bit blown away by all this news, especially as it was mostly incorrect. I hastened to say, when she gave me time to speak, 'Actually, Mr van Bruern is here to meet my aunt, Mrs Bartlett. And I don't think Rick is considering a new job, Allegra.'

She looked dumbfounded, but said quickly, 'So I've got it wrong, have I?

Well, I must go at once and correct my informant. Can't be spreading news that's not right, can I?' And off she trotted, looking very upset, while I continued on my way, grinning a bit and wondering who had spread this tale of Rick leaving town. And hoping, at the same time, that it really was incorrect.

* * *

We were ready and waiting at noon the next day, Aunt Cis dressed up in what had once been a very smart two-piece costume, and still looking good on her, with a white blouse setting off the dark blue. I played safe with a plain shirt and well-cut trousers in grey, topped with a grey jacket and a very lovely vintage scarf. I thought we must appear attractive to this Mr Bruern, whoever he might be. He arrived on the dot of twelve, in what Aunt Cis whispered to me was an old Bugatti motor — years old apparently, but in tip top form, with shining chrome and glistening leather upholstery. We locked the door behind us — Nigel, of course, having other things to do — and then smiled into his friendly, lined old face.

'Ladies,' he said, 'what a pleasure this is. Please seat yourselves . . . now, allow me to help, Mrs Bartlett . . . ' And then we were off, driving slowly but, I thought, pleased with the image, rather elegantly through the town and halting outside the King William, where a friendly car park attendant jumped to service as soon as he saw the gleaming old car.

Inside the hotel, with its thick carpets and shining mirrors, we were welcomed and taken to a private room with a table already laden with damask napery, silver cutlery and crystal glasses. Nothing too good for Sebastien van Bruern, I thought, amused, but impressed too. Seated, we were offered choices of drinks before the menu was handed to us.

'Sherry, I think, if you please,' said Aunt Cis with a quick glance at me.

I said, obediently, 'Just some orange

juice, as I have to work this afternoon, thank you.'

Then, sitting comfortably with our drinks and some nibbles, Sebastien started to talk in his lovely soft accented voice. He said, 'The young man, Rick Martin, who contacted me about your silver swan, Mrs Bartlett, will be here to share luncheon with us. I thought it right that, as he is my informant, he should know exactly what I have discovered.' He looked at the watch on the chain dangling across his chest. 'He should be here at any moment.'

I felt very heartened to know that Rick would be here to share what Sebastien had to tell us. And to know that whatever the news, Rick would be still interested in our silver swan. Which meant, I hoped, that, despite Charlie, he might still want to see me . . .

When he arrived, I was astounded for he looked quite different. His long hair had been cut, and his shabby clothes replaced by a smart, colourful shirt, what looked like new Chinos, and a well-cut jacket of dark green checked wool. I know I stared, for he looked at me and grinned, saying for my ears alone, 'The new look — hope you approve?' And then offered his hand to Sebastien who was on his feet and looking him up and down.

I realized then, that the 'new look' was a well thought out ploy to impress this expert. And of course, I remembered the Craft Competition was taking place quite soon, so perhaps looks mattered? I did approve of the new look, and resolved to tell him so, if we had the chance to be alone together at the end of this important lunch. But then I wondered if it had been Charlie who had persuaded him to try and look tidier? If so, I thought darkly that she didn't understand the strange world of creative artists, and I hoped Rick's shortened hair would soon grow longer, and resume its lovely arty look. I told myself rather huffily that I, too, was a creative artist, and knew what I was talking about.

But then we sat down to our meal, and the serious talk began. Sebastien finished his grilled steak, looked across the table at Aunt Cis, and said, 'You are wondering about the history, and, indeed, the value of your little silver swan, Mrs Bartlett. And I am here to tell you what I know. But first I must tell you that in the late eighteenth century a famous silversmith in Austria made a series of small animal pieces, one of which was a swan. They sold well, owing to his name, but over the years no trace of them has been seen. So, of course, when I saw your little swan, I wondered at once — and — ' He bowed across the table to Rick sitting beside me. 'And your knowledgeable young friend, too, wondered if the last piece had finally appeared in today's world. I did a lot of research, in books, in papers, on the internet and so on, and have to tell you that, alas, I still don't have the last piece in the jigsaw puzzle. This might be the famous swan, or it might be just one of many copies made by amateur craftsmen hoping to make a quick pound or two. So I must ask you to wait a little longer, as I have one final colleague to consult who has a fuller library of silver marks than I have.'

He looked at Aunt Cis with what I saw was sincere apology in his hazel eyes. And I saw how she had suddenly paled, but even so quickly recovered control over her thoughts, as she said, 'It's clear that you have been extremely thorough in your investigations, Mr van Bruern, and I can only thank you for all you have told us. For myself, I never truly thought the swan was valuable — it had been a little lucky charm in my childhood, and I was content to let it remain so. But in these days it has become important to value everything, and so I was happy to let my family do what they could to discover the truth.'

He looked at her and I saw how warm his expression was. He said gently, 'You are a very sensible woman, if I may say so, Mrs Bartlett. And as you are happy to let me continue my investigations, may I persuade you now to try one of the delectable desserts that are on the menu?'

Which brought laughter and a lowering of the charged atmosphere. So we all had creamy puddings, and Sebastien engaged Rick in a silver-based conversation, with the outcome that he would drive us back to the shop and then go and visit Rick's workshop before returning to spend the night in the King William and then drive back to London first thing tomorrow morning.

After that sumptuous and enjoyable meal — coffee of course, to end with — Sebastien and his Bugati took us home, and we waved what was almost a fond farewell from the shop door, seeing him drive sedately up the hill and out of sight.

And I was left thinking about the swan — still no real news — and then, perhaps most importantly to me, about Rick, who had whispered, as we left the hotel, 'I'll see you soon, Mel — don't give up hope, will you? Just keep your fingers crossed.' He gave me a warm smile as I nodded and sighed and watched him walk down the street towards the river.

14

Nigel, I thought, was behaving even more strangely than usual. He was off to work the moment he cleared his breakfast plate, appeared briefly at lunch time and demanded a cheese sandwich with some of Aunt Cis's excellent chutney, then rushed off, not appearing again until just as we were dishing up supper and wondering if he had disappeared for good.

I asked him a few leading questions: 'Who is the chap with the costume jewellery stall who is teaching you all he knows?' And then, more carefully, 'And have you learned much about silver, then, Nigel, since you've been working so hard?' But neither of them brought any really sensible answers.

'Geoff Baker does the costume jewellery. And as for silver, well, I haven't really learned enough yet to branch out as a silver expert myself, but I have hopes. Every day brings something new, you know, Mel.' And so I had to be content with that, busying myself with my own sales and acquisitions, and making sure that Aunt Cis's ankle was really healing.

Since that luncheon with Sebastien van Bruern, I had taken care that the silver swan, which Rick had returned to me, was hidden in the bottom drawer in my bedroom, wrapped in winter jerseys and safe from prying eyes and searching fingers.

The days went past very quickly, and suddenly we were reminded by notices around the town that the Craft Competition was only a few days away. It was to be the culminating event in the Fair which always took place in mid summer, a celebration of the medieval past of the old town, involving some old ceremonies and jollifications. Despite being quite busy with the increasing sales of vintage clothes, I had felt slightly downcast when time passed and

Rick had made no effort to come and see me. I had been so sure he would appear, wanting to talk about Sebastien's visit to his workshop, and telling me whether anything exciting had come from it. But no word. Well, I thought, that's men . . .

Then more resolutely, I accepted that he had his work to do. And Charlie to see whenever time allowed. Why on earth should I expect him to come and find me? I put all thoughts of men out of my mind, and instead planned how I would acquire an autumn range of vintage clothes, as the demand appeared to be increasing and September would soon be here.

And then, unexpectedly, one late afternoon, as Aunt Cis was closing her shop and I was thinking about making a cup of tea for us both, Rick appeared. He came in at the back kitchen door, having knocked lightly, and at once came to my side. 'Putting the kettle on, Mel?' His smile was warm and my unhappy thoughts of not wanting to know any more men instantly died.

I smiled back and said cheerily, 'Of course. It's the one time of the day when Aunt Cis and I can relax and discuss our customers.'

'You're both busy, are you? And your aunt is recovering from her fall?'

She came into the kitchen at that moment, and he swung round. 'I hope you're better, Mrs Bartlett, because I plan to take your niece off for the evening — can you spare her?'

I'm sure my mouth dropped open, because Aunt Cis chuckled, as she said, 'I am much better, thank you, Rick, and yes, Mel has my permission to disappear for a few hours. But bring her safely home, won't you?' She gave me a loving smile. 'I should miss her company, you see ... she's a very special person.'

He turned from her, and looked into my wide eyes. 'I think she's special, too — so, Mel, will you come out for a bite this evening?'

And I, surprised, simply nodded, but

also nearly dropped the tea caddy I was holding. 'I — er — strong tea, or weak? And you don't have sugar, do you?'

I could see from the expression on his face, and those twinkling blue eyes, that he thought my embarrassment was very funny. So I tried hard to control my foolish thoughts as I made the tea, and say something sensible. Which came out, in a rush, as, 'Has Mr van Bruern given you a commission? Are you going to London to work for him? Will you miss the Fair next week?'

He perched on a stool, pushed the milk jug towards me and arranged three mugs in a row by the teapot. 'Answers in order — one, no, he hasn't given me a commission, well, not yet, but he did hint at something; two, no, I'm not going to London; and as for missing the Fair, you bet I'll be there. I've never missed one yet. Anything else you want to know?'

I shook my head, my wits in a dither. What a fool he must think me. And then I realized we were going out together later on, and that made me give him a big smile. 'Nothing else,' I said, 'and sorry I was so silly. So where are we going this evening?'

He watched Aunt Cis pouring tea and smiling her secret smile, as if she found all this chat amusing. Then he said, 'Wherever you like, Mel. Tell me and I'll take you there.' He turned to Aunt Cis, nodded slightly, and said very gently, 'And I'll bring her home safe, Mrs Bartlett — not too late. You can trust me, you know.'

We drank our tea quietly, and began chatting idly about what to expect at the Fair, when Nigel arrived, barging into the kitchen and looking askance at us. 'Goodie!' he said, grinning. 'Time for tea, and I do hope you've made some more biscuits, Aunt Cis. I had no lunch, and I'm starving.'

I said nothing, but thought all the more and avoided Rick's eyes. What must he think of Nigel? I wondered. And then remembered that they had already had a difference of opinion, so I looked at Aunt Cis, and we exchanged glances, which finally made me say, 'There's cheese and ham in the dairy, Nigel. And you know where the breadboard is, so you'd better see what you can do to appease your ever hungry appetite. I don't suppose Aunt Cis will be cooking much for her supper as I shan't be here, you see.'

He looked at me sharply. 'Really? Where are you going, then?'

I wanted to shout at him, but restrained myself, and said coldly, 'I can't tell you. We haven't decided yet.'

'Ah!' He sat on the end of the table, eating a biscuit, and looked at me very keenly. 'So obviously, the important question is really, who are you going out with? Couldn't be this chap here, could it? Not the clever clogs who knows everything about silver?'

I caught my breath, but had no chance to reply, as Rick said, slowly, and with his voice under tight control, 'I don't know everything about it, I'm afraid. But probably a lot more than you do. And where Mel and I go is hardly your business, I think.'

Silence, while the two men looked at each other with what I fancied were sparks in their eyes. I feared feelings growing into a proper row, so said quickly, 'Nigel, do go and find something to eat — perhaps when your appetite is appeased you'll behave a bit better.' And then I looked at Rick, and said, 'Shall we have another look at the stable outside, Rick? I think Aunt Cis has had second thoughts, and is more inclined now to think it might indeed make you a good workshop . . . finish your tea and let's go outside.'

We put mugs down and headed for the door, while Aunt Cis engaged Nigel in questions about how his new career was going. I breathed a deep sigh of relief as we stood out in the yard, and Rick said, his eyes searching my face, 'That oaf gets to you, doesn't he, Mel? Apart from him behaving like a bad-mannered school boy. Why is that, I wonder?'

I stood there for a long moment, and then found an answer. 'Because I don't trust him, Rick. He's one of those guys who never sticks to what he's doing — and I'm afraid he's capable of doing something that might affect Aunt Cis, even perhaps lose the shop for her. And I can't let that happen.'

He put his hand on the stable door, and stood there for a second or two, before looking back at me, and then asking, very quietly, very gently, 'And you need to trust everyone, don't you, Mel? And especially the men in your life.'

I felt my breath start to race and tried to turn away, but his arm went round me and I could no longer avoid looking into those enquiring blue eyes. I knew I had to tell the truth, so I said, a bit unsteadily, 'Yes, Rick, that's so. Trust means everything to me.'

H nodded, as if he understood, but how could he know about Tony leaving me and so causing my lack of trust? I tried to switch off my thoughts, but he was too quick for me and changed the subject. For even as he smiled again, he moved away, opened the stable door, and said, 'Let's have a look at the windows. That'll be the biggest problem, if your aunt does agree to my coming here.' And we went into the shed, and then we were talking about the need an artist has for the best possible light.

In the gloom of the shed I felt less confused about my feelings, so it was a shock when Rick said, just as we were about to leave, 'Mrs Bartlett's change of heart is good news, Mel — but I have to ask you — a little while ago you imagined Charlie would be moving in here with me. Well, I do hope that idea doesn't still worry you.' He paused, and I saw his eyes narrowing a bit, as he added slowly, 'And there certainly won't be any other girl moving in, Mel — I can assure you of that. So does that remove your own second thoughts about my coming here?'

We stood close to one another, so

close I could feel his breath, sense the tension in his mind, but what could I say? Rick was an attractive, vibrant and kindly guy who would surely attract lots of other girls. But why was he so sure he wouldn't want to have a partner with him here as the years went on? I had no answer ready, so turned away, saying unsteadily over my shoulder, 'Now you're asking personal questions and I'm not ready to answer them, Rick. And anyway, let's go in and talk to Aunt Cis about the conversion, shall we?'

I knew I shouldn't have said that about personal questions, but I wasn't ready to tell him what was in my heart. Just in case I couldn't trust him . . .

So we talked about the possibility of converting the stable into his new workshop, and I left him and Aunt Cis discussing costs and rentals while I went upstairs and thought about what I would wear for the jaunt out this evening. Something a bit less plain and solemn, perhaps. Not the dark trousers I usually wore, but a vintage pleated skirt the shade of apricot, which swirled about my legs, with a silk top that picked up the shade in a richer colour. I held the clothes up to me and looked in the mirror, thinking that I looked better than usual. And it was important, for some reason which I couldn't really sort out, that I looked my best to go out with Rick this evening. As I went downstairs again, I wondered what that reason was; why should I want to look attractive tonight? But — and I didn't understand why — I didn't dare answer the question, and so went into the shop just as Aunt Cis was closing her door, and Rick was making tracks for home.

He looked at me as he went out of the kitchen door and said, 'I'll be around to collect you — shall we say seven, Mel? And where would you like to go?'

The answer jumped into my mind at once. 'The pub by the river. We could sit under those lovely old trees . . . '

I saw his eyes light up, but all he said was, 'Your wish is my command, princess. See you later, then.'

He was in the street, heading for home, when suddenly Nigel came rushing out of the kitchen door. 'Hang on!' he shouted. 'Want to ask you a favour . . .'

Rick turned and I saw from his expression that he was finding it hard to be polite. I thought I heard him say, 'What is it?' I couldn't hear more, but I saw him listening carefully as Nigel, close to him now, went on and on. I thought, if this is a favour, it's a long one, but decided not to make an issue out of it. Nigel would always be his own peculiar person, and I must put up with it. I must trust him; as I supposed Rick was doing.

So I went to Aunt Cis and we chatted about her sales during this past week, and when we might do the shopping, and how much better was her ankle? And then she said, 'Make sure you enjoy yourself this evening, my dear. I think Rick is a trustworthy man, you know, so make the most of him, why don't you? And what are you going to wear?'

I told her about the skirt and the silk shirt, and she nodded her head. 'So go up and give yourself time to wash your hair and really look pretty. Up you go.'

Her cheeriness made me smile, and I went up the stairs two at a time, planning to do just what she said. For yes, I intended to enjoy myself this evening — with Rick.

15

He was there on the dot and I was ready, waiting impatiently, for a swirl of excitement was working itself through me. Just a big smile, a wave from me to Aunt Cis, and we were off, walking down the street towards the river. After looking at me with thoughtful eyes, and seeing how my smile increased, he nodded, took my hand, and together we swung along, not speaking, but, I thought and hoped, of one contented mind.

Before we reached The Anchor Inn, by mutual consent it seemed, we found a bench and sat down, close to the river, side by side, our eyes fixed on the gently rushing waters, green and blue and streaked with sunlight where it drifted through the trees overhead. At first we didn't speak, not until suddenly his hand shot out pointing at something flashing down the river.

'Look!' His deep voice surprised me and I bent forward to make sure I knew what he was pointing at.

'A kingfisher!' I caught my breath, for the brief sighting of the bird was so brilliant, so seemingly magical, that I knew no words could do it justice. And then it was gone. I sighed, sat back, turned and looked at him, feeling a sudden need to talk and share things as memories surfaced.

His eyes were steady, looking at me with such warmth, that words came easily. 'We used to come down here when I was a child, and there was always a kingfisher,' I said slowly. 'I had forgotten, but things are coming back now.'

Again, he took my hand. 'You were happy then, Mel.'

It wasn't a question but, surprised at his perception, I needed to reply to it. 'Yes,' I said. 'And then life began to play tricks. Like it does.'

He nodded. 'And for me, too. A bit of

a rackety growing up, and this urgent need to find my vocation. Parents not always helpful — but you probably understand.'

I was reassured by the warmth and strength of his hand around mine. Yes, I did understand, and the fact that his adolescence, like mine, was unsteady and not always happy, reassured me. I looked deeply into those cool, pale eyes, and then said, 'My parents were killed when I was a teenager. And so Aunt Cis became everything to me. Until I went to London, and met Tony.'

'Ah,' was all he said, but I knew he understood. And I was able to go on, a bit unevenly, but suddenly so thankful that I could let it all come out.

'We split,' I said. 'Too much business for both of us and not enough time. It didn't work. He left and somehow I sorted myself out, learning to be single again. Like, I supposed, he did. But — '
I stopped. This was abruptly very painful. But the pressure of his strong hand on mine helped. I gulped, then

somehow went on. 'And he found another partner. Very quickly. Too quickly, I thought. I mean, could he really have loved me, if it was so easy to forget and start again?'

'And that's where you told yourself men weren't to be trusted. I understand, Mel.'

We sat there silently now, hands held, the sun's colours slowly changing from fiery reds and golds into drifting shades of turquoise, pale blue, grey, indigo, all reflected in the moving waters beside us.

I felt different; as if I had left something behind. And it was such a good feeling. Then he moved, stood up, drew me with him and put an arm round my shoulders.

'Confession is always a good thing, Mel,' he said, his deep voice very quiet and peaceful and helping my still jumping nerves to quieten. 'Thank you for sharing your life with me. That means a lot, as I hope it does with you.'

There was a question there, and I

had no difficulty in smiling, nodding my head, and saying, 'Indeed it has, Rick.'

We stood for a few moments longer, together, watching the water, enjoying the sun's sinking rays, and then, together, we walked on towards The Anchor, and went, away from the peace and quiet, into noise and companionship. But we smiled at each other as we found a table away from the crowd, decided what to drink and then looked at the menu. I thought it was like coming away from dreamland and finding ourselves in a new world. And I knew I was enjoying it.

There was music and chatter all around us, and my spirits rose as I realized that Rick, like me, was having a good time. We talked about Aunt Cis and her ankle, and her determination to recover; and he said, 'Willpower is an amazing thing. I need it sometimes to stick at my work, wondering all the time if what I'm making is good enough to sell.'

That surprised me. The bracelet he

had made for Charlie was surely a wonderful example of his talent and craft. I asked, 'So what are you working on now?'

He looked at me quizzically, as if wondering whether I was being serious or not. Then he must have seen from my expression that indeed, I was, for he fumbled in his jacket pocket and took out the little notebook which I recognized. 'Have a look and tell me what you think,' he said. And grinned, adding, 'I'm open to criticism, so you can be quite honest.'

He laid the notebook on the table between us, and flipped open a few pages. Towards the end of the book I saw Charlie's new sketch and the outline of the bracelet. Then some small stars which ended up in a big, splendid brooch; and then another sketch of my own face just above a drawing of our silver swan. I was silent, feeling enthused with warmth, as I realized that my new sketch was smiling; and I realized not only was he very serious about the swan, but perhaps me as well? I turned, met his gaze, and saw in his eyes a demand for truth. I said, a little hesitantly, surprised that he should have sketched me again, and so differently, 'I think your work is excellent, Rick. I don't know anything about silver, but — the bracelet and those dear little stars — and your sketch of our swan, well, they touch my heart.'

He was silent for a moment, and then he leaned a little nearer to me, and said, very softly, 'And my new sketch of you, what do you think of it? You have a warm heart, Mel, and I wanted to record the lovely soft expression.'

I felt my blood start to surge. But his frankness required me to answer, so I said, 'I'm very glad, Rick, that you think I'm improving . . .'

He laughed then and pressed my hand. 'I'm not talking about improvement, but you and your warm heart. And I wonder what in particular touches your warm heart, Mel. Isn't it time for you to tell me that?'

At a loss, I felt colour rising in my cheeks. I felt foolish, but somehow excited and aware of something wonderful happening. Could I tell him that he had begun to fill my mind? That I was beginning to be aware of a new sense of trust growing inside me? Should I say these things?

And then suddenly a hand on my shoulder, a familiar voice saying, too loudly, 'Thought I'd find you here, you and your silvery friend. Well now, aren't you going to ask me to join you?'

Nigel, beside me, holding a glass of beer and looking slightly glassy about the eyes. I sucked in a deep breath and was just about to say 'No, I don't want you anywhere near me, thanks,' when I heard Rick's chair scrape back and, turning, I saw him stand up and move to stand at Nigel's side. His face was expressionless, but the cool eyes had become steely.

His voice was controlled, deep and quiet, as he said, 'This is a private outing, and I'm afraid you're not welcome.'

And then Nigel began to argue, saying something about, 'But you promised to let me have them, and so far nothing's arrived. I don't think much of your promises . . . '

I was bewildered at what was going on. Nigel stood there, swaying slightly, his face growing ever redder and Rick keeping his face expressionless. But I had heard, in the depth of his voice, a warning note and I guessed that he was becoming very angry.

I stood up jerkily, wondering what to do, but Rick had cleverly taken Nigel aside into the shadowy space below the window, and was talking quietly to him. I wished desperately that I could hear what he said, but the room was full of other voices, and all I could do was watch the two men, and hope that in a minute the spat would be over.

Yes, of course I wondered what on earth Nigel had been talking about, but all I thought of at the moment was that I wanted to be out of all this, somewhere quiet, where I could be with

Rick and stay away from problems.

And then Nigel shouted something rough and inaudible, banged his glass down on the nearest table, and stormed out of the inn.

Rick turned back, met my startled gaze, and came back to the table. He sat down and we looked at each other for a long, thoughtful moment. Then he said, quietly, and with the hint of a smile, 'Quite a storm in a teacup. I'm sorry about it, Mel — this was to have been a happy evening, but that oaf rather messed things up, didn't he?' He refilled my wine glass and the smile showed its usual glorious warmth. 'So let's drink to Nigel very soon finding a job he's good at and disappearing, shall we?'

I felt myself cooling down, settling back into the lovely calmness that our evening, so far, had brought with it. But one little worry remained. I looked into his eyes, and said very quietly, 'He talks a lot of nonsense, poor old Nigel — so what was he meaning about promises?

Do you and he have something in mind?'

I watched the smile dim slightly, but his voice was as calm as ever, as he said, 'He told me he wants to learn about researching silverware, and I promised to give him a couple of out of date silver mark books. They'll help him sort out makers' names, dates and where they were made. Not a big deal, he could always buy them himself, but I thought it easier to give him my old copies and get rid of him.'

'I see. And that's good of you, Rick. But you haven't given them to him yet? According to what he said . . . '

'No, not yet. I had them ready, but thought I'd wait until tomorrow.' An almost invisible frown appeared on his forehead, and he bent towards me. 'Too much on my mind this evening, Mel. I hope you understand?'

I thought I did. But I wasn't sure. Something about the spat between him and Nigel still clouded my mind. I sat back in my chair. 'I don't know. And I think perhaps it's time for me to get back to Aunt Cis. Shall we go?' I pushed back my chair and got up, and he did the same. But the joy of the moment had gone and I felt a new coolness growing between us as we left the inn and started walking back beside the river.

We walked in silence and I felt a terrible sadness hit me as I recalled how happy I had been not long ago, walking beneath these trees, and looking forward to being with Rick for a whole evening. Because now something had come between us; I felt it and longed to escape, but could think of no way of doing so. It wasn't just that Nigel had made an unwanted entry into our lives, but that the shadow of knowing, or perhaps just imagining, that something was going on between Rick and Nigel, stayed where it was. Even growing bigger as my thoughts went on. I needed to be at home, talking things over with Aunt Cis, and I felt my footsteps grow in length as the need grew.

Until suddenly, in the shade of a large, splendid oak tree which spread shadows over the river and the small, narrow path on which we walked, Rick stopped, turned to me, and said, 'I know the evening's gone a bit wrong, but I'd promised myself that one part of it should be right, and this is it; Mel, I want you to know that I love you. And dare I hope that you feel the same about me?'

His arms were around me, and the imaginary troubles and problems faded like a dust cloud in a shower of rain. All I knew was that he loved me, and I could honestly reply yes. I moved in his embrace, and he drew me tighter. His face was very close and I could see his eyes, pale as ever, but glowing like silver within the shadowy night. I let out all the taut breath in my body and slid my arms around his neck. Yes, I loved him. I wanted him to kiss me, and never let me go. I closed my eyes and waited to feel his lips. They were soft, gentle, and warm. And so amazingly exciting. We stood for a long timeless moment under the old tree, and I felt all my tension sliding away. Everything was working out happily. But kisses can't go on for ever, and so we drew apart, smiling, and even laughing, and then talked quietly about plans for the future as we walked back along the path towards the town.

'The Craft Competition and the Midsummer Fair at the weekend, sweetheart,' Rick said as we stopped outside the antique shop. 'And, of course, news from Sebastien. I've a lot of work to get ready, and I guess you have, too. But we'll be together as much as we can. And Mel — ' He drew me to him for a last embrace. 'Think about how we both feel, and what we should do next. Being in love, you know, is a serious matter . . . '

We chuckled quietly, and I gave him a last kiss before going indoors and locking the door behind me. Knowing it was, indeed it was the most serious thing in my life. But the cloud remained in my mind as I went to find Aunt Cis. Such a horrible thought — even loving Rick as I did, could I really trust him?

16

I dreamed — of course I did after that amazing evening — but there were bad dreams, too, and I was glad when early morning brought me back into reality. With the Fair just days away I knew there was a lot to do, not just with helping Aunt Cis prepare her stall but with making sure I had some flyers printed advertizing my stall, even though I wouldn't have one at the Fair. I wanted time to enjoy myself, as well as help with the antiques.

At breakfast I let out a few hints about Rick which had Aunt Cis smiling and looking at me with hope on her face. But she was appalled to hear about Nigel making such a nuisance of himself. The smile died, and she said, almost to herself, 'Oh dear, whatever will he get up to next?'

And then the phone rang. Sebastien

van Bruern's warm, husky voice greeted me in a friendly way before asking to speak to 'the lady who owns your little silver swan'.

I took the handset into the kitchen. 'Mr van Bruern,' I said, and heard the excitement in my voice. I couldn't bring myself to leave the room, but just got on with putting breakfast dishes into the sink, while trying to make out the conversation on the phone. But almost at once I heard the change in Aunt Cis's voice and turned to look at her.

The warm smile was disappearing, but she remained cool, as usual, and I guessed what she had just heard. She said 'Yes, most disappointing, Mr van Bruern, not the one we had hoped it might be, then, but at least we can keep the swan as our family lucky charm. No, I shan't be selling it. And I can only thank you for all your interest and work.' Her voice lightened, and a small smile played about her mouth, as she added, 'I hope we might see you down here in Devon again some time? You will always be welcome . . . '

I looked down at the washing up water and automatically cleansed a couple of plates, feeling as if my heart had fallen down to my feet; for it was quite clear that the swan was not, after all — and even with two experts researching its history — the one that the world was still waiting to find. Just a small, family lucky charm . . . but I had the control and the sense to dry my hands and go and put my arms around Aunt Cis who had sat down, looking rather unsettled. 'Never mind, Aunt,' I said, trying to put some warmth into the words, 'we never really thought we'd make a million, did we?'

She responded with her own indomitable strength, smiling up at me. 'No, dear child, we didn't. And now we can just relax a little — too much excitement isn't good for old ladies like me, you know.'

We laughed, just a bit brokenly, but then I said, 'I'll go and bring it downstairs. It can sit where we can see and admire it, and cast its luck all around us! Sit still, Aunt Cis, I'll be down again in a minute.' My mind was in confusion as I went up to my bedroom — all our hopes gone; no million pounds coming in to help with my business plan; but did it really matter? Surely the swan itself was the real prize? That helped me to come to terms with the mingling thoughts, and I opened the bottom drawer, unwrapped the winter jersey — and then gasped.

The swan had gone.

I collapsed on the bed, still holding the jersey and trying to work out what had happened. Rick had returned the swan to us, and I had carefully hidden it up here. Aunt Cis, of course, knew where it was, and then — Nigel. His name burst into my mind with growing anger and certainty. The wretch! He must have explored my room while I was out, and then found it. And taken it. Stolen it . . .

Anger helped my confusion to sort itself out. I must break the news to

Aunt Cis, and then I must find Nigel, accuse him, and bring the swan back home. I would go now . . . now . . .

Aunt Cis took the news with her usual calmness, but I could see she was hurt. After all, as she was always telling me, Nigel was family, and this was a terrible thing to have to accept. But she insisted on going into her shop, opening up and declaring that she would be quite all right on her own.

Only — 'Try and understand why he's done it, Mel, my dear. He must have a reason, you know, and perhaps even now he's on his way back with the swan.'

I said a disbelieving yes, of course, and then went out into the town. Nigel would be somewhere up near the market, so I went straight up the hill, looking in every shop window as I went, not really expecting to see our swan, but knowing I must be aware of every possible thing Nigel might have done. I found him on the jewellery stall, talking to a pretty girl who was trying on gemstone earrings, and laughing with her as he held the mirror for her to see her reflection. When he saw me his grin faded and he put down the mirror. 'Hi, Mel.' And then turned to the girl, frowning. 'Come again when you've made up your mind, will you, love? Got to do something else right now . . . ' She went off in a huff and I was left alone with him.

'Nigel,' I said quietly, 'I want to know what you've done with our swan. And why you took it. And why you should do such a vile thing to Aunt Cis, who is so good to you. So come on, talk, because I can't wait to hear your excuses.'

He looked pale and uncomfortable, but as usual he blustered. 'Come off it, Mel, no need to be like that — I only took it because — ' I watched an uneasy grin spread over his face. 'Because your chap, Rick whoever he is, asked me to do so. We did a deal, you see, some of his old books for your silver swan. I expect he's got a few ideas about what he'll do with it, so I can't help you there, but for goodness sake stop looking at me like that. Anyone would think I was a murderer or something . . . '

I gritted my teeth and tried to control my fury. 'In my mind you're worse than that,' I managed to spit out. 'Taking advantage of Aunt Cis, who's so good to you — and me — and doing such a despicable, sneaky thing. Well, you've just got to give the swan back. Where is it? Tell me, now . . . ' He took a step back and gladly I saw an expression of quick fear on his face. But he stuck to his story.

'I told you, that Rick chap's got it. No need to go on at me like this — he's the one who should take the blame.'

Of course I didn't believe him. But I knew I must go and tell Rick what had happened, listen to how his voice reacted, watch the expression on his face . . . I didn't believe that he was part of Nigel's beastly plan, but — but. I sighed as I turned away and headed for the river. There was always a but in my mind, wasn't there? Would I ever learn to be wholehearted about things — and men?

I walked very fast down the hill to the river, my mind churning with thoughts, with excuses, with facts that were all jumbled up and didn't help me to come to a decision. Rick and I had said we loved each other last night; and now I was full of doubts. He would never have agreed to Nigel's rotten deal if he truly loved me, would he? But perhaps there was something I didn't know; something he would quickly and easily tell me, which would solve the whole thing and let me realize I'd got it all wrong. Something which would send the shadows flying, and end up with me in his arms.

And then that awful but came again, sticking its painful nose into all my thoughts. I went to the workshop and said hi to Gary who looked up, smile of welcome dying as he saw the expression on my face. I strode down to the back of the workshop and there was Rick, sleeves rolled up, hair already a bit less tidy than the other day when he met Sebastien van Bruern. He was engrossed in his work, didn't see me until I stood at his side, and then he turned, smiled, slowly put down the tool he was using and said, 'Mel — what's wrong? What's happened?' Standing up, he took my arm and steered me to a chair right at the back of the room. 'You look as if the world's come to an end . . . ' His voice was light, amused, but concerned. We sat down, close to one another, and he looked into my eyes. 'Tell me, sweetheart — go on, tell me.'

Now the moment was here, I froze. Words didn't come. All I could do was to look into those perceptive, blue eyes, which were holding my gaze. I breathed in a huge breath and tried to say all that was in my mind, but the only thing that came out were trembling, too shrill few words of condemnation. 'You stole our silver swan.' And then I just stared at him, watching, wondering, longing to run from this terrible, painful situation.

For what seemed an age he said nothing, and yes, I saw his face slide out of his radiant smile into something that I feared was akin to guilt. He leaned towards me, took both my shaking hands and held them firmly in his. His voice when he spoke was quiet, but the resonance seemed to strike right through me.

'Mel, this is a load of rubbish. What are you saying? And how has it come about? Take your time, love, but try and tell me sensibly, calmly . . .'

From somewhere hope came, pushing aside all the fears and the terrible doubts. I swallowed the lump forming in my throat, focused for a few seconds on the warmth of his hands around mine, and then said, 'It was Nigel. He took the swan from where I had hidden it, and he — well, he told me you and he did a deal, your old books for our swan. He didn't know why you wanted it, but I thought — I thought — ' I came to a dead end. What I thought was too terrible to talk about.

Rick nodded, remained silent. But a smile began to lift his lips, and gradually spread all over his face.

At last he said, very quietly, 'You thought I had heard from good old Sebastien that the swan was the missing one, that it was worth at least a million, that I intended to sell it without saying a word, at the same time pretending poor old Nigel was — as usual — to blame. That's what you thought, my beloved girl, wasn't it?'

I gasped. Again, no words came. But deep within me something began to unknot. He was behaving as if everything was all right. I had no need to doubt, to fear, to accuse. Slowly, oh, so slowly, I, too, managed a very small smile. And then, finally, and with enormous relief, I knew what to say.

'Rick, I didn't know. I didn't mean — I was so worried — and so I thought — well, all the wrong things . . . I'm so sorry. So Nigel must still have the swan. And I have to find it. Oh Rick what a fool you must think me!'

I slid my hands out of his grasp and hid my face. But gently he drew them down and put his arms around me. 'Yes,' he whispered, with a loving smile on his face, 'but such a beloved fool. Now, come on, cheer up, action is what's needed.'

We stood up, smiling at one another and walked to the door. 'Go home and tell your poor aunt that all will be well,' he said.

I nodded. Watched while he said something to Gary, and then led me out of the workshop. We started walking towards the town, and I said, 'What are you going to do, Rick?'

And he looked at me with a strange new expression on his face that made me almost feel sorry for my wretched cousin.

'Find Nigel, return the swan to your aunt, and get everything sorted out.'

17

The morning of the Midsummer Fair
dawned full of hazy sunshine, and I
felt yesterday's unhappy thought and
words flying away as I took Aunt Cis
— resplendent in her new flower-
patterned dress, and with hardly a limp
to be seen — to the stall she had decided
to set up for the Fair. Everything must
go well today. And I would allow no
more buts to hamper my happiness.

In the field beside the river, the home
of Midsummer Fairs since medieval
times, a sense of energy filled the air
with trestles being put up, a bouncy
castle and a maypole erected, and the
usual ram roast already alight in a
corner sheltered from wind and rain.
And people talking, laughing, hurrying
about. Not to mention the local jazz
band, warming up.

A huge tented pavilion covered the

far end of the field, and I saw glimpses of local and visiting craftsmen carrying their exhibits into it. A great thrill ran through me as I remembered that Rick would be one of them. And then thoughts of Nigel pushed through my contentment; where was he? Where was our swan, and — my stomach suddenly knotted — had he and Rick met, faced each other and sorted out the problem of the swan? Or was it still waiting to happen?

I was busily helping Aunt Cis to arrange the few pieces of porcelain and glass she had brought with her, when Sue Bennett came to my side. 'Hi, Mel,' she said with her warm smile. 'Hoped I would see you. I have a proposition to make to you.' She paused, exchanged a welcome with Aunt Cis, and then turned to me again. 'Well, it's not my idea, but I'm stuck with organizing it, and I wondered if you would be interested in helping.'

I smiled at her. 'Just tell me how much work it entails and then I'll let you know!'

She laughed. 'Of course. Mrs Sothern wants to have a mannequin parade in her ballroom in aid of the History Society, of which she's a patron. And history includes clothes, so I'm going to find a few suitable bits and pieces, and perhaps you might do the same?'

I stopped fiddling with some pieces of glass and looked at her. 'Sounds interesting. But why can't Mrs Sothern do the organizing herself?'

'You mean you haven't heard? I thought all Stretton knew! Charlotte is going to be married in a few months to some rich guy in London and that means so much work that Mama can't spare a moment other than for wedding dress, flowers, bridesmaids, invitations, photographs ... but of course the History Society do must go on.'

We laughed together and for a few moments my mind expanded. A cat-walk in that handsome ballroom; people watching, enjoying the clothes, and perhaps wondering where they might go to find other, similar, beautiful old things. Yes, I would definitely help. And then bells rang in my head, as I realized that Charlie Sothern wasn't after Rick, after all . . . .

So I agreed to help, and Sue went away with an even bigger smile on her face. And as Aunt Cis now was organized, I said I would wander for a few minutes. It was in my mind to look about for Nigel who surely must be here somewhere. Even to search other likely stalls for a possible sight of our swan. And, most important, to wait for Rick to come and find me before the Craft Competition took place just before lunchtime.

I looked everywhere for a small silver swan shining in the sunshine, but didn't find it. I watched the school children perform their maypole dance, saw the smiling toddlers falling about on the bouncy castle, and went to see the ram, roasting and crackling, with members of the Royal Women's Institute busily buttering baps ready for the big meal. The smell was wonderful, and I lingered a bit, thinking hungry Nigel would be sure to come and buy his pounds' worth. But he didn't. And no sign of Rick.

I was on my way back to Aunt Cis to report on things, when Allegra Smith came bouncing up, caught me by the arm and pulled me beneath a shady tree. 'Ah, Melody,' she said, her smile just visible beneath the huge, flower-laden hat, 'I want to see you. Need to know where that distant cousin of yours has got to. I have news for him, you see. Yes, a possible situation . . . can't be certain, of course, but hopefully . . . well, where is he, do you know?'

I looked at her, and said, very carefully, 'Not at the moment, but he's sure to be around somewhere. I'll tell him you want to see him when we do meet. Er — what sort of job would it be, Allegra?'

She beamed. 'Oh, a really good one. Of course he'd have to leave Stretton, but I suppose that wouldn't matter, would it?'

I concealed my smile. 'No, Allegra, it wouldn't matter at all. I think he would welcome a change, actually — '

She nodded, patted my shoulder, said, 'Oh, those lovely old clothes of yours, I must come and buy something soon — when I have time — but I'm so busy . . . ' and rushed off through the gathering groups of people.

Slowly I walked back towards Aunt Cis's stall, beside the river, beneath the whispering foliage of the huge trees, and wondered what would happen next in my life. The day was certainly, so far, full of surprises, and quite nice ones. But what I wanted so badly was to have Rick at my side, and the silver swan in my hand. Would it happen?

I was half way through the crowded field when I saw him: Nigel, talking earnestly with the man who sold old silver on a stall slightly set apart. I felt my heart begin to thump. This was the moment. I ran towards him, pulling him towards me when I reached the stall. I saw his face contort, and spat out all the words which were almost choking me. 'You told me a lie! You said he had it, but of course he hasn't got it — you've still got it, you wretched creature, and now I suppose you're trying to sell it!' I turned to the owner of the stall, staring at us wide-eyed, and said rapidly, 'The silver swan isn't for sale, so you can just forget all about it.' I turned to Nigel again. 'So give it back, now, now . . .'

I waited, hand held out, glaring at Nigel, who was pale-faced and tight-mouthed, looking at me as if I was about to eat him for dinner. 'I — ' He began the usual blustering, but I wouldn't let him give me any excuses.

'Just give me the swan, Nigel,' I said very sharply. But then, watching him closely, I saw how he suddenly looked over my shoulder, and so I swung round, finding myself close to Rick — who, I realized, looked as angry as I felt. I stepped away, aware that everything was about to be sorted out by these two guys. I had no part in it, but deep anxiety coursed through me. What would happen next?

I sensed Rick's fury, but was amazed at the control in his deep voice, as he said, 'Hand it over. You've done enough damage trying to make something out of what's after all, just a small family heirloom with little value. So give it back to Mel.' His voice hit a sinister bass note. 'And quickly.'

I saw Nigel sweating, eyes going from side to side, as if seeking an escape route, and then, abruptly he turned and ran down the field, towards the river. And then I saw Rick following him.

I stood there as if turned to stone. What should I do? It was the stall holder's amused voice that told me the answer. 'Reckon he'll give it up, or else end in the water — Rick Martin's a heavy chap to argue with, you know . . . ' And that made me move, running, following them both through the field, praying that no one would end in the river — and specially that the silver swan wouldn't disappear for ever in the mud under a meter or so of fast flowing water.

When I reached the riverside path I realized that people were gathering. Of course — Fair day and perhaps this was a jolly bit of comedy theatre to amuse them all. But to me it was the exact opposite of comedy — I saw Rick and Nigel facing up to one another, heard the rumble of Rick saying something sharp and short, and Nigel's high-pitched voice shouting a reply, but then their arms were flailing, the audience began shouting for the winner — whoever it might be — and both men, now fighting, edged nearer to the water. Then the fight stopped abruptly. I saw Nigel fumble in his pocket, find something, throw it at Rick and then turn and run away. But he slipped on a root of one of the big trees, and lost his balance.

There was a huge splash, and I gasped, for Nigel was in the water, arms reaching up, shrill voice shouting for help, and then — I could hardly believe it — another, even bigger splash, and

Rick was in the river, too, one hand held above his head as he managed to pull Nigel towards the bank. The crowd loved this; laughter, cheers for the winner, and then they cheered even louder as Rick — still holding something in one hand — heaved him out onto the path, where he lay like a stranded whale. And all this time I stood, as if frozen to the spot where I was, watching, wondering, hoping, fearing, and now — I hardly like to admit — laughing with the rest of the watchers.

For Nigel got to his feet, looked about him, pulled a terrible face, and ran, dripping, along the path and finally out of sight. And Rick, also dripping, but smiling, wrung out his sodden shirt tails and sleeves and came to my side. Clasped in his wet hand was the silver swan. He held it out towards me, a wonderful smile lighting up his blue eyes.

'I think, like your beloved cousin, this needs drying off and finding a happy resting place. Here you are, Mel.'

I took it, the silver swan, wet and cold, and so in need of attention and love. Warmth surged inside me and I didn't know what to say. But I took the swan and smiled at Rick, and hoped he understood that words weren't enough. He must have done, for he smiled back, touched my cheek with a wet finger, and said, quietly and just for my ears only, 'That's one of your problems solved, sweetheart. So go and tell Aunt Cis while I dry off and find clean clothes — the Craft Competition will be starting fairly soon. I'll see you there, shall I?'

'Yes. Of course I'll be there. With you.' The only words I could summon, but they said exactly what I was feeling. I watched him walk away, with cheers from the watching crowd trailing after him and then made my own way through the field, to tell Aunt Cis that her family heirloom was safe and would never roam again.

And as I went, new thoughts came

waltzing into my mind; happy thoughts, hopeful ones. An image of him keeping the swan safe, even as, soaked through, he rescued Nigel, lifted my whole being. For I knew now, that, as well as loving Rick, I could trust him and, suddenly, life was full of promise.

I kept my own promise to Rick and found a seat in the pavilion when the time came for the Craft Competition to be judged. I was well at the back, but I saw Mrs Sothern in the front row who, when she turned to look around, saw me and waved. So she remembered me — and the vintage clothes, I hoped. Sue Bennett came and sat next to me, smiling and warm as ever. 'Fingers crossed for Rick to win,' she whispered, and I agreed with all my heart.

But it wasn't to be. The judge, a famous craftsman from up country, said many complimentary things about all the entries, but clearly it was the wooden carved shield with Stretton's coat of arms on it that held his fancy. Although he complimented Rick on the delicate chain pendant with an embossed swan hanging from it. And he smiled, as he turned it over in his hands, and then looked at the audience.

'A fine piece of work, especially with the crystal eye of the swan, and initials carved small and delicate beneath it. And, let me say, a private inscription carved on the back — but not my prize piece, after all. So let's take another look at this handsome carved wooden shield, which honours your town's past and has to be my downright winner.'

My heart sank, of course it did. But could it really matter? Rick's work had been noted and highly praised, and there would be other competitions in the future. And the fact that he had used the silver swan to make a pendant was all that mattered to me. A pendant; with initials on it: my breathing grew fast, as I started counting the minutes that must pass until he came and showed it to me. The afternoon drifted on with eventual packing up of stalls and taking down maypoles and bouncy castles. Everyone was busy, and laughter and chatter filled the field as I helped Aunt Cis pack up her few antiques and then took her home.

'What a happy day,' she said with a big smile. 'I didn't sell many things, but it was wonderful to see how well everything went.' She looked at me very lovingly. 'And you, Mel, my dear? Of course you're disappointed that Rick didn't win the competition, but at least he has saved the swan for us. Oh, and I almost forgot to tell you — I saw Allegra Smith rush up to Nigel — yes, he appeared again during the afternoon, dried off and looking a bit dazed — and then lead him off to meet someone. So it really looks as if that elusive job has finally turned up!'

And then, as if on cue, he came into the kitchen, all smiles, and obviously in a hurry. 'Hi!' he said with the widest grin I've ever seen. 'Guess what? I'm off to Exeter for an interview — I've wangled a lift with someone driving back there — you see, this firm is looking for a guy with ideas, and well, that's me! I'll go and get my things and then I must fly — he's waiting outside.'

Aunt Cis and I looked at each other, and I know relief and amusement filled our faces. Then he came downstairs again, hugged her, gave me a brotherly kiss, and said, 'Can't stop — I'll let you know how I get on, and, oh yes, thanks for having me . . . ' and disappeared, our chorus of 'Good luck, Nigel' following him.

We had a peaceful cup of tea and finished up the last flapjacks and then Aunt Cis said happily, 'I think I shall have a nap now — too much excitement, you see — and I expect you have your own plans for the evening, Mel . . . '

I answered the question in her voice with a smile and a nod. No need for words. She knew what I was planning.

Later I walked down through the town, quiet now and peaceful with sunset colours lighting up everything they touched. Beside the river the big trees stood, shady, still and powerful, and I found the usual bench and sat down. The water sang as it flowed past me, and I thought how wonderful it was, just to sit, and wait among all this natural beauty.

But I didn't have to wait long. A footstep behind me, warm, strong arms around me, a kiss on my lips as my head turned, a kiss that was sweet and loving, and lasted until our breaths ran out, and then Rick came and sat beside me, hands around mine, blue eyes shining and looking deep into mine.

'Are you disappointed that I didn't win? But does it matter, sweetheart? And I have something which, I hope, will make you feel better. Mel, this was made for you.' Out of his jacket pocket he drew the pendant, and put it on my lap.

I gasped, and stared. Such a delicate silver chain, and hanging from it a square piece of silver, embossed with a small swan. As the swan's eye caught the fading sunlight and flashed up at me, I felt my whole body relax into a huge sense of wonder and joy. And below the swan, a tiny lover's knot formed out of our initials, M and R. And, as if that wasn't enough to send pleasure pounding through me, on the back of the pendant were two words which made my joy overflow.

Love always.

Tears pricked behind my eyes as I put my arms around Rick's neck and drew him close, knowing that I had found love, and that this time it would go on — and on.

THE END

We do hope that you have enjoyed reading this large print book.

Did you know that all of our titles are available for purchase?

We publish a wide range of high quality large print books including:
Romances, Mysteries, Classics
General Fiction
Non Fiction and Westerns

Special interest titles available in large print are:
The Little Oxford Dictionary
Music Book, Song Book
Hymn Book, Service Book

Also available from us courtesy of Oxford University Press:
Young Readers' Dictionary
(large print edition)
Young Readers' Thesaurus
(large print edition)

For further information or a free brochure, please contact us at:
Ulverscroft Large Print Books Ltd.,
The Green, Bradgate Road, Anstey,
Leicester, LE7 7FU, England.
Tel: (00 44) **0116 236 4325**
Fax: (00 44) **0116 234 0205**

SUZI LEARNS TO LOVE AGAIN

Patricia Keyson

Upon meeting troublesome pupil Tom's father, Cameron, young schoolteacher Suzi feels an immediate attraction. She is determined not to be drawn into a relationship, knowing she would feel unfaithful to her late husband; but the more time Cameron and Suzi spend together, the more they are captivated by each other. Suzi rediscovers deep emotions, though she agrees with Cameron that Tom must come first . . . But how long can Suzi hide her love for Cameron?

THE DUKE & THE VICAR'S DAUGHTER

Fenella J. Miller

The Duke of Edbury decides he must marry an heiress if he is to save his estates. So far he has managed to stay out of the clutches of the predatory mothers who spend the Season searching for suitable husbands for their daughters. The god-daughter of his aunt, Lady Patience, might be a suitable candidate, and he is persuaded to act as a temporary guardian to both her and her cousin, Charity Lawson. When Charity and Patience exchange places, the fun begins . . .

A PLACE OF PEACE

Sally Quilford

When Nell participates in a transatlantic house-swap, going to stay in New England on the beautiful Barratt Island for three months, she hopes to escape the shame she left behind in Derbyshire. She soon meets gorgeous police chief Colm Barratt — and scheming socialite Julia Silkwood, whose husband's health seems to be failing suspiciously quickly. With Nell's overactive imagination running riot, and her past about to catch up with her, she fears she could lose Colm forever.